Morning Mist of Blood

A Novel by

Eric Wilder

Other books by Eric Wilder

Ghost of a Chance
Murder Etouffee
Prairie Sunset
Name of the Game
A Gathering of Diamonds
Over the Rainbow
Big Easy
Just East of Eden
Lily's Little Cajun Cookbook

ISBN: 978-0-9791165-3-7
Gondwana Press LLC
Edmond, OK 73013

I wish to thank G. Terry Felts for his technical advice, tips on forensics and police procedure. I also want to thank Logan County Sheriff Jim Bauman and Captain Bill Warner, and Oklahoma Deputy Sheriff Gary Kinney for their help.

For Marilyn

Morning Mist of Blood
A novel by
Eric Wilder

Prologue

Three men on horseback stared up at a stark sky and rustler's moon. Howling coyotes had spooked their horses and one of the men ran a calming hand down his mare's neck. The noisy creatures could do little harm to the big horse, but she didn't know it.

The man's loose denim jacket didn't quite fit around his barrel chest and did little to protect him from the cold. It didn't need to as his anxiety kept him warm. Removing his cowboy hat, he raked thick brown hair out of his eyes and wiped a bead of nervous sweat from his forehead with a red neckerchief.

Coyotes didn't worry the man but another sound did, riveting it along with the slow burning fire in his gut. Some tortured creature was crying out, its tormented moans echoing through the darkness. Agonizing whimpers of intense pain stopped abruptly following a muffled pop.

"What in the cornbread hell was that?"

"Sounded like someone skinnin' a hog that weren't quite dead yet. Maybe we ought to do our business some other night."

"Shut the fuck up, Shorty. It was probably just some kids spotlighting coyotes with a .22."

Shorty wasn't so much short as he was skinny. His scraggly black mustache didn't quite hide his sunken cheeks, wracked with acne scars. He stroked his chin and shook his head.

"Didn't sound like no coyote to me and that sure weren't no .22."

"Don't matter. We're here now so let's get what we came for."

He slapped his horse's rear and she started forward, out of central Oklahoma's thick underbrush and into a clearing leading to a neat fencerow. A grove of trees, an effective windbreak for some of the rancher's cattle, occupied the other side of the fence. The man already knew this.

"Ready for me to cut the fence?"

The dark-haired man asking the question was younger than the other two and had a crooked frown that made him seem even more so. The worn Stetson pulled low over his forehead and his day-old growth of beard failed to mask his baby face.

"Don't have to cut it. I rigged it so we can get in and out without anyone being the wiser. We may want to steal a few more head sometime and there's no sense in tipping Clayton off to the spot where we're gettin' in at."

Sliding off his horse, the man with the baby face found the reworked fence post. After pulling the section back and laying it on the ground, he remounted his horse and followed the other two through the breach.

The rustler's moon provided all the visibility they needed and they soon found a small herd of special cattle situated for the night. Something had spooked them and they were pacing in a narrow circle. When the lead man spotted a darkened silhouette near the pond, he held up a hand and dismounted, not worrying his well-trained mare would bolt. He approached with caution what looked like the crouching silhouette of a man.

"What is it?" Shorty asked when he returned.

"You were right about the skinning, but it ain't no hog. It's a dead man in a pool of fresh blood."

"Sweet Jesus," the baby-faced man said.

"Stow it, Johnny. Let's round up the cows and then get the hell out of here."

Shorty and Johnny knew from the irritated tone of Garth's voice not to ask any more questions. Skirting the little herd of cattle, they turned them toward the breach in the fence. Unusual for wintertime central Oklahoma, no wind was blowing. The cattle stirred, unhappy with yet another unexpected disturbance. Shorty slapped a cow on the butt with his hat and it started toward the breach. The others followed her, soon leaving only an owl as witness to the theft.

Shorty waited until the last cow had disappeared into the blackjacks before resetting the hidden gate, and then followed Garth and Johnny into the stunted undergrowth. He soon left the moon's muted glow. It was then they heard another eerie sound—a marauding panther, coughing softly to let everything around it know he was on the prowl.

Shorty's horse trotted forward, directed only by instinct as the earth began to drop downward into Skeleton Creek, a narrow canyon fully thirty feet below the area's normal elevation. The deeply dissected gully disappeared into shadows as he hurried after Garth and Johnny.

Spooked, the cattle continued voicing their alarm, their hooves clattering against cobbles in the dry streambed and echoing against steep walls of the narrow canyon. No light penetrated the thick mass of tree limbs encasing the deep void that seemed almost like a dark tunnel. The three men had an answer, treading their way by the spare illumination of headlamps they wore on their hats. It was all they needed.

The canyon followed a straight line for almost a mile. No one, even were they near, would have detected the presence of the rustlers, their mounts or the lowing cattle thanks to the foliage-covered tunnel. As the three men herded the cattle up a steep trail, out of the creek, moon and starlight made their path seem like Broadway on New Year's Eve compared with the eerily lit tunnel they had just exited.

Up ahead, an oilfield tank battery's slow-moving pumping unit sang an out-of-key tune with its moving rods. A cattle trailer attached to an old Ford pickup awaited them, along with a newer Chevy and horse trailer. Shorty dismounted without bothering to tie his colt. Opening the trailer's rear gate, he yanked out a ramp so Garth and Johnny could begin herding the cows into it.

"We got too many. They ain't all gonna fit," he said.

Shorty's words didn't make Garth happy. "Then make 'em fit."

Shorty began pushing the cows into the trailer, trying to force them all in. The last cow just wouldn't go.

"Ain't gonna happen," Shorty said.

Garth dismounted, turning the cow away from the cattle trailer and out the breech in the fence.

"We don't need this one anyway. You can see it's the wrong color. Heeyah!" he shouted, slapping the beast with the back of his hand. "Get the horses in the trailer and let's vamoose."

"Won't that heifer tip us off?" Johnny asked.

"Nothing we can do about it now and she'll probably be a long way from here by morning."

Morning Mist of Blood

Garth and Johnny led the horses into the second trailer and stored their gear in its tack room. They watched as Shorty drove through the open gate and onto the section line road, not following until he had disappeared with a rumble.

As the truck and trailer drove away in a cloud of dust, the frightened cow glanced around, trying to decide what to do next. The low growl of a nearby panther did little to comfort it.

Chapter 1

Buck McDivit exited the heavy glass doors of the Second Bank of Edmond, trying without success not to feel like someone had just kicked him in the gut. His banker, a man he had known all his life, had just rejected his request for a new truck loan.

"You got no steady job and not much in the way of assets. I can't risk the bank's money on this one," he had told Buck.

Buck had stared at the little man with a voice much deeper than his size indicated and tried to reason with him. "I've never had a loan go south. You know as much, Jeb."

"Things change," Jeb Stuart Johnson had said, peering over his reading glasses. "The auditors would have my ass in a sling if I made this loan. Unless you put twenty percent down, that is."

"I don't have that kind of money."

"Then maybe you don't need a new forty thousand dollar pickup. You know what the monthly payments are on a loan that big? Hell, Buck, what's the matter with the truck you got?"

"Two hundred thousand miles," he had replied. "Maintenance is eating me up."

"Then lower your standards because you can't afford a truck costing forty-two grand." The little man whisked his hand through his thinning hair before glancing at his watch. "Now I got another appointment coming in right after lunch so I'm leaving a little early. Anything else I can help you with?"

Buck didn't bother answering because Jeb Johnson had already grabbed his overcoat and headed out of the office. He pulled the collar of his jean jacket up around his neck and followed him through the front door to Broadway, Edmond's main street.

Buck's boots were old but always polished and well maintained. He had long legs and his jeans and Western shirt made him seem taller than he really was. Two women passing on the sidewalk turned to give the handsome young cowboy with expressive brown eyes and dark wavy hair a second glance. Still upset about his meeting with Jeb Johnson, he failed to notice.

Edmond, a former train stop had grown into a north suburb of sprawling Oklahoma City. No longer a bedroom community for the wealthy, it was now the home of the third largest university in the state. It was also the third largest city in Oklahoma.

The thriving little metropolis had traffic that didn't quite rival Dallas but was on its way to doing so. It also had a hundred fifty churches and at least ten Starbucks. Cold gusty wind whistled down the street, chilling the back of his neck, as someone tapped his shoulder.

"Sorry to bother you, Mister but I ain't ate in two days. Can you spare a dollar?"

The economy, as in other parts of the country, had begun collapsing in Oklahoma. It seemed beggars populated every major cross street in the City but this was the first one Buck had seen in downtown Edmond. The man was scruffy, his clothes dirty and torn, but it was his dog that caught his attention. The man held on to it with a short strand of rope tied around its neck.

The young black and white Border collie wagged

its tail and licked Buck's hand when he reached down to pet it. He fished out his wallet and glanced at his last twenty.

"What's your dog's name?" Buck asked.

"Ain't got no name."

Buck handed him the twenty. "I don't have anything smaller so I guess it's your lucky day." He pulled the bill back when the man reached for it. "You have to promise me part of this will go to feed your dog."

The little man snatched the bill from Buck's hand and stuffed it into his shirt pocket.

"He ain't my dog. I was gonna tie him to a park bench and be rid of the little pest. If you want him, you better take him cause he ain't staying with me."

Buck frowned, thinking for a moment he should take back his twenty. He took the rope instead and watched the ratty little man hurry away, probably to the nearest liquor store.

He squatted and rubbed the little dog's ears. The dog with no name wagged its tail and licked Buck's hand.

"Maybe I can put an ad in the paper and find a good home for you."

Feeling suddenly depressed because of his loan rejection, he wondered if he should move north to Logan County and the less pretentious town of Guthrie. Someone he recognized exited the coffee shop across the street, interrupting his malaise. Waving, he crossed the narrow street, the dog wagging his tail as he followed him.

Unlike sprawling Oklahoma City, no skyscrapers jutted into the clouds in downtown Edmond. Few structures, if any, exceeded more than two stories in height, those mostly squat brick and native rock buildings. The people walking along the sidewalks moved at the slow pace of what was once a small town.

Clayton O'Meara, his ex-employer and the former

husband of Virginia, the woman for who he now worked, had apparently not seen him and was heading in the opposite direction. He stopped when Buck called his name.

"Trying to avoid me, Clayton?"

Clayton grinned, showing a set of teeth a little too perfect for someone his age. He stood several inches taller than Buck, probably six foot four, and he sported a full head of silver hair, complete with expensive salon highlights.

"Hey, Buck. Nice leash you got. What are you doing up so early?"

"I was about to ask you the same thing?" he said, ignoring Clayton's comment about the dog's makeshift leash.

Clayton answered Buck's question with little more than a wry grin and the word, "Business. Don't you ever feed that dog?"

"He's not really my dog."

"From the way he's wagging his tail, I'd say he thinks he is."

A wealthy oilman, Clayton O'Meara owned a large cattle spread in southern Logan County. He rarely left the showplace ranch and Buck couldn't recall ever seeing him in downtown Edmond. Despite the chilling temperature, the older man wore no hat, probably so as not to distract from his full head of hair. Only an unzipped orange goose down parka emblazoned with the letters OSU covered his designer sports shirt.

Clayton was at least thirty years older than Buck but the sparkle in his hazy eyes made him seem little more than a teenager. Glancing at his Rolex Commander, as if the expensive watch somehow held the answer to some unasked question, he pointed to his car down the street.

"I'm sort of in a hurry."

Buck recognized a brush-off when confronted with one and said, "Didn't mean to hold you up."

Clayton grinned and slapped Buck's shoulder. "Sorry to rush, but I got an appointment and I gotta get. We can catch up on things later."

Instead of hurrying away, he turned toward the door of the coffee shop he had just exited. Reaching for the handle as if he had forgotten something inside, he thought better of it. Pivoting on the heels of his polished snakeskin boots, he headed down the street to his awaiting vehicle. Buck watched as Clayton's chauffeur opened the back door of a big white Mercedes for him. With tires squealing, the car hurried away, around the corner.

Buck glanced at the door of Café Oklahoma, the coffee shop a fixture in downtown Edmond for almost as long as he could remember. He knew Clayton well enough to know he wasn't a coffee drinker. Curious, he opened the door and glanced inside.

Seeing a familiar face alone at a table, he completely forgot about Clayton as memories of a recent romance, ended too soon for his liking flooded his psyche. It was his former girlfriend, Kay Karson. Everyone called her KK. She turned around, as if expecting someone else. Seeing him, she folded her arms, frowned and glanced away.

"No greeting for an old friend?" Buck asked as he approached her table.

KK crossed her shapely legs, black lace hose and ankle-length boots the only concessions to the outside chill, considering the short leather skirt she wore.

"You're really full of yourself, aren't you?"

Before Buck could answer, an employee said, "Sir, you can't bring your dog in here."

"I'll only be a minute," he said.

Buck and KK had been an item for almost a year. She liked line dancing, prancing horses and ice-cold Coors beer. Her slender legs looked great in tight blue jeans and cowboy boots. Honey blonde hair draped her shoulders, framing her slightly less than perfect but unforgettable face. She was, in fact, a beauty queen, having amassed three titles before the tender age of eighteen. Buck soon learned she thoroughly realized the effect she had on men. Now, at twenty-nine, she could focus her power on the opposite sex like an ICBM, with the same explosive result. Buck had found his dream woman. At least he'd thought.

KK's father was a medical doctor in Tulsa, her mother a college professor at Tulsa University. She had never wanted for anything. Looking at her now, Buck could see she had acquired a few very expensive trinkets he doubted even her doting dad could afford. A diamond pendant graced her slender neck. The large diamond in an expensive setting had good color and was no fake. It was a companion piece to the diamond ring on her finger sporting an even larger and more ostentatious stone. Mink lined her gloves and the expensive jacket draped across the back of the booth.

"Just saying hi to an old friend," he countered.

KK tipped over a half-empty coffee cup with her elbow. Dabbing at the spot with a napkin, she continued frowning.

"You call yourself an investigator. You don't have a clue. I imagine you must have thought all you had to do was smile at me and I would jump back into your bed like a horny teenager. Well, we're not in college, and you are not the star quarterback and campus heartthrob anymore. You don't even have a real job. You may have a nice ass but it doesn't compliment your lousy future."

KK didn't wait for his reply, brushing past him and appearing not to hear when he said, "Guess tamales and dancing Saturday night are out of the question."

As she disappeared out the door without looking back, he wondered what he could have done to provoke such a display of anger. With a shrug to the employee still looking at him and the dog, he followed her outside, watching as she entered a brand new white Mercedes sports car, pulled out of her parking place and gunned away down the street.

"No problem," he called out at the disappearing vehicle. "I can't afford a date Saturday night anyway."

Two rejections and a brush-off before noon, he thought as he considered where she had acquired the Mercedes and her expensive mink jacket. Their relationship had not ended badly. It had simply flickered out and died.

Buck had attended college for a time at OSU. He had dropped out to sign on with the OCPD. One of his friends there had left to become an oil and gas lease broker during one of the many oil booms, and he soon followed him. His lucrative job ended during an unexpected, at least to him, reduction in oil prices. Since then, he had supported himself in many different jobs such as club bouncer, skip tracer, process server, and private detective. His opportunities for gainful employment had recently narrowed and he found himself using his meager savings to pay his bills. It didn't help that his aging Dodge pickup needed repair almost weekly.

"Come on, Buddy. Let's get you something to eat."

When Buck reached his truck and unlocked the door, his cheeks burned hot. He'd never had an ego problem, even though gorgeous women often became speechless when meeting him. It didn't matter because now he needed a drink, preferably something with whiskey in it. Shaking his head, he remembered he couldn't afford one.

It was past lunchtime, his stomach growling. After stopping at a convenience store, he began searching for change in the truck's console.

"You wait here. I'll be right back."

He returned a few minutes later with a hot dog. Giving the meat to the young dog, he ate the bun. The little border collie gobbled down the wiener then curled up and went to sleep in the passenger seat.

Buck had not reached the horse ranch where he lived and worked part time when he received a call from the Logan County death investigator. One of his many jobs included assisting the investigator whenever a suspicious death occurred. He did not care for the often-gory work. It didn't matter now. Because of his current financial situation, he could ill afford to turn down a job, no matter how distasteful.

A cowboy had discovered a body at a nearby ranch. Clayton O'Meara's ranch. Buck pondered the coincidence as he turned his truck around and headed north, along with his sleepy passenger.

Chapter 2

Muted sunlight peeked through a thick cover of clouds as Buck stood in a semicircle with a group of men, waiting for the arrival of the death investigator. Not knowing what to expect, he let the young dog out of the truck. He was curious, but kept his distance from the men. After checking the perimeter around the truck, he wallowed a spot and stretched out to observe the scene.

No one spoke as a gray van backed up to the location. Probably already a banner day for homicides in Logan County, the person exiting the van was Satchel Pratt instead of Doc Watson, the usual man for the job. A chill wind whipped tree limbs at the nearby ranch house. It didn't matter to Satchel Pratt, his only protection from the weather a light jacket imprinted with the words death investigator. Satchel's horn rims did little to impart an air of studiousness to the large man with dark hair pulled back in a ponytail.

"Nice dog, Cowboy. What's up?" he asked Buck, ignoring the other half-dozen law officers and ranch hands standing around, waiting for something to happen.

"A dead cowpoke needing your expertise."

Understanding fully he was being bull-shitted, Pratt smiled and tapped Buck's shoulder.

"I'll do my best," he said.

Clayton's large ranch was several miles west of the I-35 corridor, the mournful horn of a distant semi barely discernable. Buck could see the house, barns and many outbuildings through a mist rising up from the pasture. A grove of stunted trees north of the fencerow marked the course of Skeleton Creek, the deeply incised streambed filled with water only during rainy parts of the year.

The interstate highway came out of Dallas, heading north through Oklahoma City and Wichita. Local law enforcement usually had a field day along the route, intersecting tons of illegal drugs coming from Mexico. Crows flying overhead voiced their displeasure with the disturbance going on below. Buck also noticed Clayton's cows, herding up in anticipation of their dinner. They seemed to sense something horrible had happened and he wondered if the dead man was the person that usually fed them.

No one had approached the body, wary of destroying evidence at what was obviously a gruesome crime scene. It was the body of a male, his legs bent at the knees and folded beneath him in what would have been a most uncomfortable position. If he were alive to notice. He wasn't. A crumpled felt Stetson covered the man's face and one of the deputies took a step back when Satchel removed the hat. Opened wide, the dead man's eyes stared back at them. Buck guessed the person's age at mid-forties, his dark hair and moustache yet to show any gray. He was slender and seemed in good physical condition, other than what had caused his demise.

The first job of a death investigator is to check for trauma, something causing the inopportune death. Sometimes trauma is not apparent. No such problem existed with this death. The man was quite naked and lying in a puddle of blood pooled mostly beneath his buttocks. Satchel Pratt pulled on a pair of rubber gloves and knelt beside the victim. From his black bag, he removed a syringe he used to extract a sample of blood from the victim's femoral artery.

Pratt had a sheath on his belt from which he took what looked like a meat thermometer. After labeling the blood sample, he deftly inserted it beneath the right side of the man's rib cage, directing the instrument into the dead man's liver. The lead cop, a Logan County Sheriff's deputy, stepped closer.

Satchel wiped off the thermometer with a cloth and placed it back in the sheath. "Can I borrow your pen?" he asked the deputy.

The dead man's head rested in a mess of blood, bone and brains. Gently lifting it, Satchel inserted the pen into the gaping hole.

"This is the exit wound," he said.

The man's bloodless lips formed a grotesque smile, a dribble of blood on both sides of the mouth. The second stage of rigor had set in and Satchel had to open his jaws with a plastic Archimedes screw. He used the opening to probe inside with the Deputy's pen. When he removed it, he turned around and offered it back to the man.

"You keep it," the deputy said, shaking his head and taking a step backward.

Satchel grinned, one Buck had seen many times. It was all part of his shtick and he performed it for the benefit of dupes that hadn't yet observed the scene of a homicide, and for the entertainment of others that had. Zipping down his light jacket, he slid the pen into his shirt pocket. His performance not yet complete, he anticipated the Deputy's next question.

"How long has he been dead?"

Buck tried hard to keep from smiling as Satchel removed a second meat thermometer he kept sheathed on the right side of his belt. Holding it close to his myopic eyes, he touched the instrument to his tongue. Both deputies and the three cowboys, not realizing the instrument was not the one Satchel had inserted into the man's liver, gasped.

"Maybe as long as twelve hours," Satchel said, "But it could be less. It's fairly cold and I can't say with certainty."

Seeing the men's stunned reaction, Buck could contain himself no longer, breaking into an uncontrolled bout of boisterous laughter. It stopped abruptly when a familiar voice spoke behind him.

"What's so funny, McDivit?"

Buck knew without turning it was Logan County Sheriff Jim Hagen.

Buck didn't bother answering because he knew the sheriff had witnessed Satchel's little act on more than one occasion. Someone much taller than Sheriff Hagen and someone he'd already seen once that day, accompanied him—Clayton O'Meara, owner of the ranch on which the dead man was murdered. Clayton smiled at Buck and nodded.

"What's the story here, Satchel?" Hagen asked.

"Well, Sheriff, I'd say you got yourself another homicide."

Buck took notes as Satchel Pratt began to recite.

"Caucasian male, probably in his mid-forties. Someone brought him into this clearing about ten to twelve hours ago and forced him to strip off his clothes. They tied his hands behind his back with chicken wire and had him kneel. Then they castrated him—while he was still alive from the amount of blood on the ground. They stuck a weapon in his mouth and pulled the trigger."

"Sounds more like suicide to me," the sheriff said. "No one would let a shooter stick a pistol in their mouth."

The deputy snickered, but turned his head away when Pratt said, "You mean you would start resisting right after you cut your own balls off?"

Sheriff Hagen shook his head. "I'm just saying when somebody dies from a gunshot wound in the mouth, it's usually suicide. What's your take on it, Buck?"

"Whoever sliced him up took more than his balls. From the cuts on his chest, it almost looks like someone was trying to skin him alive. Maybe the murderer gave him the option to kill himself."

"Satchel, sound about right?"

"I'd say at least part of Mr. McDivit's story holds water, except the victim's hands were bound behind his back. I don't know how he could have pulled off that little trick, but then again I'm not a professional fiction writer."

It was Buck's turn to smile. Perhaps he had concocted too much of a story, but he was not the lead homicide detective, only an assistant to the death investigator who had voiced his opinion when asked.

It didn't really matter and Jim Hagen seemed to agree with Buck's theory. "What else?"

Everyone, including Satchel Pratt turned their attention to Buck when he said, "There were three men on horseback here last night."

"How do you know?" Hagen asked.

"It's getting dark and I'm not as good a tracker as my Cherokee godfather, but the ground is damp and a blind man can see the tracks."

Glancing at the big man standing beside him, Sheriff Hagen asked, "Your men?"

Clayton shook his head. "Don't have a clue, but we can ask my foreman."

"You recognize the victim?"

"Frank Boggs, one of my best hands. Been with me since I bought this ranch. He had an apartment on the place and lived here full time. My foreman can get you all the information we have on him."

Sheriff Hagen glanced at his lead deputy, still

ashen-faced from observing Satchel's little performance joke. "Get your head out of it, Lamont. Tape off the crime scene, get pictures and start combing the area for evidence. Don't look like we'll find much, but you never know."

Clayton turned to leave, shaking his head and motioning his gawking cowpokes to accompany him. He smiled and nodded at Buck before leaving. The dog had remained by the truck but kept a vigilant eye on the proceedings. He was smart and it had taken him no time at all to learn his boundaries, a quality Buck instantly noticed and appreciated. Satchel also noticed.

"One fine dog you got there. How much did you have to pay for him?"

"Twenty bucks," Buck said with a grin.

"I'll give you fifty."

"Sorry, but I'm starting to get attached."

"Yeah, what's his name?"

"He doesn't have one yet."

"Think I'd call him Pard if he were mine." When the dog's ears perked up, Satchel said, "See, he even recognizes it."

The day had started out cold and had only grown colder. Satchel was a seasoned death investigator and had already determined much more from the body than he had conveyed to Sheriff Hagen. It seemed unlikely Buck would ever see the investigation through to fruition so he didn't linger on the thought for long. As he and Satchel finished their work, the murder scene began to look like a washed-out oil painting. It was the end of a long day and wet flakes of snow began falling from an ashen sky as they rolled the dead man in a gurney to the back of Satchel's van.

Chapter 3

Buck's morning started unexpectedly with a wet tongue licking his face.

"Morning, Pard. I bet you need to go outside."

After a glance at his old Rolex, he crawled out of bed. It was still two hours before daylight. Buck lived on a thoroughbred horse farm in eastern Oklahoma County. The very wealthy woman that owned the place provided him with an apartment on the second floor of the million-dollar barn in exchange for certain daily tasks, mostly feeding and exercising the horses on the farm. Not an easy job because the big animals from time to time numbered almost fifty.

Buck didn't mind because it gave him a roof over his head. He also loved the horses and they loved him. He knew every animal by name, and also if they liked carrots, or apples. He went outside with Pard. When he finally stumbled back upstairs to the bathroom, he dabbed his face with cold water from the tap. Maybe I drank too many beers last night, he thought as he turned on the lights. Pouring a can of beef stew from the pantry into a bowl, he sat it on the floor by a second bowl he had filled the night before with water. The dog ate the beef stew and his tail never stopped wagging.

Morning Mist of Blood

Upon stepping into the shower, a warm stream of water soon dispersed his dreams and returned him to reality. By the time he had toweled the drops off his broad shoulders, he felt good as new again, or at least better than he had when he awoke.

Mrs. O'Meara's former boyfriend, a horse trainer less than half her age, had taken a new job in Kentucky. Jilted, she lost interest in her farm and began traveling extensively. Now, she was in Scotland. Buck adored everything about the thoroughbred farm, but hated fending off her constant advances. Not that she was hideous or even unattractive. Hell, she looked and acted a lot like Ann-Margret. Her recent absence from the place still came as a relief.

Virginia O'Meara had acquired the farm in a divorce settlement from her former husband Clayton. Clayton didn't mind. His passions were oil, cattle and women, and not necessarily in that order. He had only bought the farm to satisfy Virginia's whim. She was rich enough in her own right to afford it without him. The daughter of old Oklahoma wealth, she liked the trappings money brought her and cared little that Clayton's fondness for her had lots to do with a pending merger with her granddad's old-line oil company.

Buck's apartment was more than he needed with its mahogany paneling, expensive carpeting and real gold faucets in the bathroom. It also had a relaxing balcony overlooking the training track that afforded a scenic view of much of the farm. He was glancing out the window at a trainer, working a horse on the track, when the phone rang.

"Buck, is that you?"

He instantly recognized Clayton O'Meara's whiskey-wracked voice. After divorcing Virginia, the rich oilman had bought a ranch in nearby Logan County, his house more like a ski lodge than ranch house, its tall ceilings beamed with fresh hewn timbers.

American Indian art and mounted animal trophies occupied every wall, bear skin rugs the polished wood floors. Buck loved to visit, sitting on the veranda at night, sipping whiskey and listening to coyotes howl.

"What's up, Clayton?"

"Seeing you twice yesterday got me thinking. You're just the man I need to help me. Drop by the ranch and we'll talk about it."

***

After purchasing a supply of dog food from a nearby convenience store, Buck drove to Clayton O'Meara's house, only a few miles away down an unpaved section line road. Pard had taken the passenger seat as his own and stood staring out the open window, his tail in a constant wag. They found the ornate electronic gate already open, signaling Clayton was expecting him. There were guards lurking somewhere near. Usually when he visited they would hassle him unmercifully, making him wait a half hour or more before allowing him to continue down the winding road to Clayton's ranch house. Today, no one bothered him.

O'Meara employed at least thirty hands on the large spread, many of them solely for security reasons. Clayton was big on security and it had surprised Buck to see him alone in downtown Edmond without a single bodyguard. The thought crossed his mind as he passed through the gate.

They followed the narrow blacktop road through landscaped acres of manicured lawn toward Clayton's house. Cottonwood trees along the creek were leafless, awaiting spring. When Buck exited his truck, he glimpsed an armed cowboy watching him from the open loft of a distant barn.

Leaving the window open, Buck said, "Wait for me Pard. I won't be long."

Buck had visited Woolaroc, vacation retreat of oilman Frank Phillips, and Clayton's rough-hewn log house reminded him of it. If anything, it was even larger and more eclectic. He entered the back entrance of the enclosed veranda without knocking. Sipping a glass of straight Kentucky bourbon, Clayton greeted him.

"Too early for me," Buck said, waving away Clayton's offer of whiskey. "Coffee, maybe."

Clayton snapped his fingers at someone behind the door. "Seems this young man is too righteous to drink morning whiskey, Maria. Bring him a cup of coffee instead."

Clayton's house was massive, its out-of-place southern-style veranda his favorite spot. Buck could see why as he settled into a comfortable rattan rocking chair located next to the older man's leather recliner. Clayton liked anything expensive and the veranda's teak floor emulated the deck of a sultan's yacht.

An antique brass telescope and wheelhouse from a luxury riverboat sustained the nautical motif. The veranda wrapped around part of the house, including Clayton's bedroom. Its sliding glass door was ajar, a pair of eyes peeking through the bedroom curtain. Clayton had obviously just come from there, his bathrobe covering his pajamas.

Clayton had grown up in a lower middle class Edmond family and had attended OSU on a football scholarship. His PE degree had gotten him a sales job with an international cementing company's Oklahoma branch. He eventually started his own oil company utilizing the many contacts he had made as a salesperson. Clayton's primary talent was raising investor money. Raise it he did, parlaying it into a dynasty while never letting on his PE degree was in physical education and not petroleum engineering.

Buck had known Clayton for years but most of the dirt on him he had heard from Clayton's ex-wife, Virginia, usually when she was in her cups and putting the moves on him. Being an information junkie, he listened to her stories, even if it sometimes got him into trouble. He'd been able to avoid a messy situation with the amorous-minded older woman, at least so far.

Clayton's housekeeper and general assistant around the house appeared with a cup of strong black coffee for Buck.

"Thanks, Maria. You always remember just the way I like it."

Middle-aged and slightly dumpy, she smiled without replying to the compliment. When Clayton sipped his whiskey and moved to the porch swing, Buck joined him following a sneezing fit.

"Allergies?"

Buck nodded. "This time every year. At least your cottonwoods aren't blooming. When are you going to cut them down?"

"Never," Clayton answered. "You'd complain about a sharp stick in the eye."

"You know me too well," Buck said with a grin. "Maybe we should discuss your problem now."

Clayton slammed the whiskey in one gulp. "This might take a while because I have more than one."

His frown and furrowed brow indicated to Buck something was distressing him. His ranch was large by Oklahoma standards and it included llamas, peacocks and other exotic animals. He also ran a large herd of cattle. Buck sipped his coffee, waiting for Clayton to tell him what was bothering him.

"I lost a cow the other night. Sheriff Hagen thinks coyotes or bobcats are the likely culprits. He even suggested not to worry about it because I have bigger fish to fry because of the murder on my property."

"You don't think so?"

Clayton scratched his chin. "The murder is another matter and, hell, it might even be connected. Something got one of my cows and whatever did it wasn't a coyote or a bobcat. You got time to take a look?"

"Nothing on my dance card today."

Clayton grinned and excused himself for a minute, disappearing through the curtains into his bedroom. He returned fully dressed, donning his cowboy hat and wool-lined leather coat Maria had brought him, as if on cue. After a glance at the dancing curtain in Clayton's bedroom to see if someone was still peeking at them, Buck followed him out the back door where a tan Jeep awaited, its key already in the ignition.

"Mind if I bring my dog?"

Clayton grinned. "I don't mind, but you told me yesterday it wasn't your dog."

"Things change."

When Buck whistled, Pard bounded out of the truck's open window and joined them, jumping into the Jeep's backseat.

"Smart dog," he said.

The old Jeep had no top or windshield. Clayton cranked the engine and pulled forward almost before Buck had a chance to crawl in. There were no seatbelts.

"Most of my herd winters in the pastures just north of here. There are plenty of trees and gullies to break the north wind and two large ponds for water," Clayton said, driving with one hand and rubbing Pard's head with the other.

They followed a bumpy dirt road bordered for some distance by large rolls of hay. Buck could see part of the herd in the distance, mostly stout-shouldered Black Angus with a few Texas Longhorns mixed in for conversation sake. There were even a few deer munching on a lone bale of hay. A clump of blackjack trees lay in the distance and Clayton headed toward them. Pard didn't bark or miss a thing.

They stopped along the way to go through two gates, Buck stepping out of the Jeep to open them. Blackjacks bounded Skeleton Creek that had incised the mostly flat ranchland, sometimes to a depth of nearly a hundred feet. The old Jeep screeched to a halt near the edge of the trees.

Clayton stepped out of the old vehicle. "We'll have to walk from here."

Buck and Pard followed the large man down the steep slope, neither out of breath when they reached the creek bed, full of water from the recent snowfall. Thick tree growth and shadows obliterated a dull sky. They soon came to a path leading up the slope to the other side.

"Deer path," Clayton explained after sloshing across the creek and starting up the slope. "Along with every other creature you can imagine."

They dragged themselves up the final few feet of the ravine with the help of a hanging vine. Buck and Pard followed him to a clearing where they saw and smelled the carcass of a cow. Pard circled it, not getting too close.

"One of yours?" Buck asked.

"It's mine all right."

Buck walked around the dead cow, studying the cuts and slashes on its black hide.

"The Sheriff is right. Something did a job on this one."

"A big animal."

"Like what?"

Clayton paused only briefly before answering, "I think it's a panther."

Buck had heard tales all his life from farmers and ranchers in the area about their panther sightings. Most were only slightly more credible than having seen a UFO. Still, belief in the presence of big cats in central Oklahoma persisted and the wounds on the carcass of Clayton's cow did nothing to belie the legend.

"You didn't bring me here to see a dead cow. What else is on your mind?"

Clayton grinned. "I didn't want to talk about it back at the ranch."

"I'm listening."

"I started noticing about a month ago I'm missing some cows."

"Very many?"

"No, just a few."

"With the size of your herd, how in the world would you know if you'd lost one or two?"

Clayton nudged a red sandstone rock with the toe of his boot, and then glanced up at the morning's gray sky.

"Every animal has a numbered ear tag. We use the tags so we'll know if they get their shots, keep tabs on how old they are and so on. The information's in a computer database and there's not much I don't know about my herd. I think you can help me find out what's going on."

"You have thirty hands on this spread. You don't need me."

Clayton pointed to a slow-moving pumping unit in the nearby clearing. "See that oil well over there? One of those storage tanks holds about two-hundred barrels, about fifteen grand worth of oil at seventy-five dollars a barrel. All a thief has to do is drive on the lease at three in the morning, back a bobtail up to the spigot, fill it and drive away. Oil is virtually untraceable. You can't tell one barrel from the next. It's a perfect crime."

"What's your point?"

"My point is there's never an oil theft without a company man knowing about it. The pumper gauges every tank, every day and knows how much oil is in each one of them. Oil thieves don't drive up to a random oil well and chance being caught robbing a tank with only a few barrels in it. They usually work with the company pumper who tells them which well to hit. The oil thief has a nice payday and the company man gets a cut."

"You think one of your hands is involved in the theft of your cattle?"

"Not just my cattle. I think someone is

systematically stealing crude from Crescent Oil."

"Any ideas?"

"Someone that knows about my cattle and oil business."

"Can't be very many people."

"Nope, just one. Roy Dunlap, the President of Crescent Oil."

"Roy is your close friend, or am I mistaken?"

"Best friend."

"You think your best friend is stealing from you?"

"I don't know, but I intend to find out. Consider yourself on my personal payroll starting today."

"Won't Roy be suspicious?"

"He and everyone else needs to stay in the dark. I already told him you are a consultant doing due diligence for someone considering buying part of my oil and cattle holdings. You'll have access to company records and he won't know what you are really looking for."

"I'll need to get a look at your cattle database, and the employment records of all your hands."

"Consider it done. Roy is expecting you. He has an office ready and will supply you with a computer with all the information you need, including my ranch records."

Clayton grinned when Buck asked, "What else is on your mind?"

"Since you're on the payroll, you may as well help me with all my problems. You got time to listen?"

"I have all day."

"I started buying land around this ranch years ago. I managed to put together four sections. Almost." Clayton pointed toward the Cimarron River Buck knew lay just beyond a distant grove of blackjacks. "There's about two hundred acres right smack in the middle of my ranch I don't own. I've offered ten thousand an acre for the property but they won't sell."

"Who can afford to turn down that kind of

money?"

Clayton frowned to show his disgust. "A commune populated by a crazy bunch of women."

"If they won't take ten thousand dollars an acre, what can I do about it?"

"You got a way with women. Nose around and see if you can influence things for me. Even if they won't sell, I'd still like to know as much about the place as possible. Talk with the people in charge. Find out what they are up too. While you're at it, I'd like you to keep up with Frankie Boggs' murder. I don't expect you to solve it, but see what you can turn up."

"You give me more credit than I deserve when it comes to women, but I will look into it for you, and the murder. While we're here though, let's look around."

"Good, you impressed me last night with your tracking skills. I didn't know you were an Indian."

"I'm not."

Buck's Cherokee godfather had made sure he had developed a knack for tracking. The key was to look for something out of place, a footprint, a broken twig. He walked in an expanding circle around the dead cow, searching for anything anomalous. Despite the animal's wounds, he saw no sign of a struggle, not even a drop of blood on the ground.

After nearly ten minutes of silence, Clayton could no longer contain his curiosity. "What do you think?"

Buck shook his head. "Whatever killed your steer must be a ghost."

"You're kidding?"

Buck glanced up from the ground and slowly scanned the surroundings. Seeing nothing out of the ordinary, he followed Pard, sniffing at a nearby clump of bushes. Sinuous vines, lined with sharp barbs, formed an almost impenetrable mass of undergrowth. Buck grabbed a bush, revealing a path when he pulled it aside.

"Good boy, Pard."

They navigated the narrow path with care, occasionally stopping to extract briars from their jeans, and soon found themselves on the edge of the ravine. The narrow path led down to the creek. Grasping vines and vegetation, Buck followed Pard down the steep path. When he reached bottom, he grabbed Clayton, sliding perilously toward him.

"You okay?"

"If we ever get out of here."

Already busy studying the creek bed, Buck didn't comment. Erosion had diverted the main course. What remained was a gravel-lined draw that took a different direction than the creek. The draw, surrounded by underbrush and the ravine's steep walls formed a nearly invisible pathway. Buck, with Clayton in tow, followed Pard until the path widened.

A pristine pool of water lay near the center of the dry channel Africans would call a wadi. Buck knelt down to get a better view of something Pard was nosing near the clay edge of the pool.

"What is it?" Clayton asked.

"A pugmark," Buck said, moving aside to give Clayton a glimpse. He pointed at the impression of an animal's footprint in the clay. "I'd say whatever made it was one big cat."

Clayton studied the pugmark, and then asked, "What's your dog got in his mouth?"

Buck took the object from Pard. "One of those LED headlamps hunters use when they're spotting game at night".

***

Clayton barely stopped talking during the short drive back to the ranch. Buck only nodded when he said, "I told you I had a panther on my place. Now maybe someone will believe me. That was a panther track, wasn't it Buck?"

"Yes Sir, it was."

"Where did it come from?"

"Big cats are free roaming so it's impossible to say. Probably just kept moving until he found a place that suited it."

"But why here?"

"You have a big spread with lots of trees, rocks and shelter, plenty of water and wild game and almost no humans around. You are a mile from a major highway and most of the section line roads dead end when they reach your property. What more could any wild animal ask for?"

"Why hasn't someone seen him before now?"

"You saw the trail where we found the track. We were probably the first humans to ever lay eyes on that little pool of water, except the person who lost the headlamp. The cat has a lair somewhere near and sleeps during the day and hunts at night, mostly for wild turkeys, rabbits and feral pigs, I'd say."

"Should I send the boys out to hunt it down?"

"He has plenty to eat without attacking your herd. Your cow was somewhere it wasn't supposed to be. I suspect it would be alive today if he hadn't been where we found it. My question to you is how did she get all the way across Skeleton Creek?"

Clayton had no answer. "I'll have the boys run the fence line and see if they can find a break."

"Have them do a head count while they're at it," Buck said. "Probably has something to do with the horse tracks we saw near the murder scene."

"Won't it tip them off I'm suspicious?"

"Just because you think someone is rustling your cows doesn't mean you believe one of your hands is responsible. Do a headcount. When you find some missing, and we both know you will, report it to Sheriff Hagen. If nothing else, it may slow the rustlers down until we can get a handle on things. We might even flush a nervous quail or two."

When they reached the ranch, Clayton pulled the Jeep next to Buck's truck and handed him an envelope.

"Your first month's wages, an unlimited credit card and keys to your company car. You'll find it in the parking garage at the Petro Place."

Buck didn't argue. Clayton had already wheeled the Jeep around and headed for the barn. The sputtering engine of Buck's truck returned him to reality, as did the sight of the expensive white Mercedes sports car parked next to Clayton's larger white Mercedes. It looked like the same car he had seen KK driving the previous day.

As he exited the open gate of Clayton's property, he pondered the implication. Pard, already taking a nap in the passenger seat, didn't share his concern.

Chapter 4

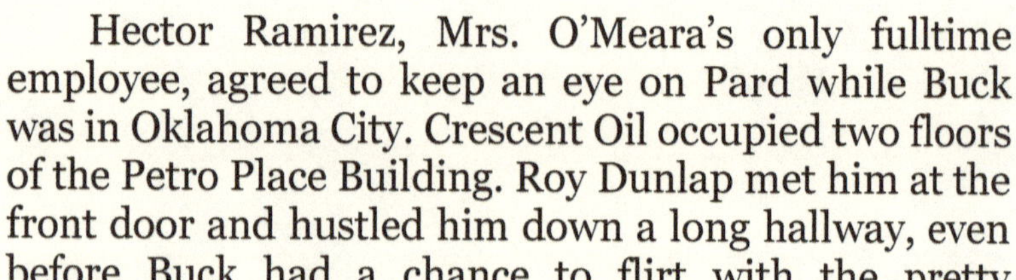

Hector Ramirez, Mrs. O'Meara's only fulltime employee, agreed to keep an eye on Pard while Buck was in Oklahoma City. Crescent Oil occupied two floors of the Petro Place Building. Roy Dunlap met him at the front door and hustled him down a long hallway, even before Buck had a chance to flirt with the pretty receptionist. Ushering him through the door of his large office, he shut it behind them.

Dunlap was probably in his sixties but even with his snowy white hair, he seemed much younger. He had youthful green eyes and kept himself thin and fit, probably playing golf and tennis. Only a loose layer of skin around his neck, covered mostly by his shirt collar and expensive tie, belied his true age.

"Grab a chair," he said, sitting behind an executive desk that must have cost Crescent Oil thousands of dollars.

He was immediately on the phone, ordering coffee from his secretary. Buck had barely settled into a leather chair when a very pretty woman entered without bothering to knock.

"Thanks, Georgia," Dunlap said, not introducing the woman to Buck.

He glanced at her as she walked out the door. More than pretty, she was stunning with stylishly short, honey-blonde hair and big eyes a soft shade of blue that seemed almost too perfect to be real. Buck noticed her short skirt and athletic legs as she exited the office. From her grin, it was apparent she noticed him noticing.

Roy Dunlap also noticed. Tapping his desk to get Buck's attention, he offered him a cup of coffee from Georgia's carafe. After a sip, Dunlap's icy stare disappeared. Inhaling deeply, he leaned back in his expensive executive chair.

"You know Clayton as well as me. I don't know anyone more interested in security than him. The company records are for no one's eyes but yours, and what you are doing no one else's business except mine and Clay's."

Roy Dunlap finished his coffee and motioned Buck to follow, leading him down the long hallway to an office near the water cooler. The office was much smaller than the one they had just vacated but appeared fully functional with desk, worktable, side chairs and even a laptop computer.

"Consider this office yours. Everything you need to know about Crescent Oil and Clayton's cattle business is on the laptop. You answer to no one here but me. I told everyone you are a temporary employee doing land work for Clayton. I'd appreciate it if you go along with the story."

After Dunlap left his office, Buck sank into the chair behind the desk. Swiveling around, he gazed out the picture window at traffic moving rapidly on Northwest Expressway. From the seventh floor window, he could see the tall buildings of downtown Oklahoma City, about five miles to the south. Because of Oklahoma's prevalent winds, it has little smog and almost no air pollution. From a building as tall as Petro Place, you could see for miles.

He still hadn't opened Clayton's envelope so he took a peek, whistling when he saw the unexpected size of his first month's check. A knock on the door interrupted his musings and he stowed it in his pocket, turning to see the broad smile of a nice looking young man.

"You must be Buck," he said. "I'm Ty. I work in the land department."

"Hey Ty," Buck said, rising to shake his hand.

"Would you like a tour?"

"You bet," Buck said, following the young man out the door of his new office.

Ty was taller than Buck and had a full head of curly red hair. His wire-framed glasses seemed more for show than necessity as he kept them propped on his head like a tiara. He was dressed semi-casually in designer jeans and snakeskin cowboy boots, along with a dress shirt and expensive tie. Clayton obviously paid his employees well.

Crescent Oil had about forty employees and Ty introduced Buck to every one of them. It didn't take long to realize whoever did the hiring had a penchant for blonde young women, every one seemingly prettier than the next. Susie, the receptionist, was probably the prettiest, but the title was up for grabs, and likely rested in the eyes of the beholder.

Buck met secretaries, irascible old geologists, world-weary petroleum engineers and fast-talking landmen. Landman doesn't imply gender, as females occupying that particular job are also landmen. Ty introduced him to Dunlap's gorgeous secretary Georgia, his attraction immediate. There was not a single minority among the employees, everyone lily white. It was almost quitting time when he finally returned to his office, Ty still with him.

"Some of us are having drinks after work at Nick's," the young landman said. "We'll be in the bar."

"Thanks, maybe I'll take you up on it after I check

a few things here."

Buck knew Nick's well, and his past consumption of their strong drinks had likely caused him the loss of more than a few brain cells. Ty's invitation was a good chance to glean information not available in his desktop database. The restaurant and bar boasted the best steaks and mixed drinks in Oklahoma, its bright red wallpaper making it look like the inside of a French whorehouse. Garish wallpaper and dark surroundings were apparently conducive to good food, drinks and conversation because the place was always brimming with happy patrons.

Ty met him at the front door and led him past the ornate bar to a couple of tables in back the regulars from Crescent Oil had pulled together. Everyone except Ty seemed preoccupied with his or her conversation, so he took the opportunity to quiz the young man.

"What's the story on Roy Dunlap?"

"Mister O'Meara's best friend. They are usually in here together. They go to football games and do business deals. Roy is never very far away."

"I don't recall Roy having that much money," Buck said.

"He does now. I hear Mister O'Meara lets him in on drilling deals on the ground floor. He's not hurting for money."

Buck remembered a story about Henry Ford, a person so rich he had no friends with whom to socialize. He fixed the problem by seeing to it several associates also became very wealthy. Enlightened self-interest. Perhaps it was Roy Dunlap's role.

He had little time to ponder Dunlap and Clayton as Susie the receptionist and Georgia joined them. Without knowing exactly how, he found himself seated between the two attractive women. Within minutes, they were both vying for his attention. Ronnie, a waitress Buck knew from the old days showed up at the table to take their drink order, plopping into his lap soon as she recognized him.

"Buck, where have you been?"

"Living north of Edmond now. I don't get this far south much anymore."

"You hurt my feelings. You could at least drop in occasionally."

"I'm working for Crescent Oil now and promise I'll be back more often."

She kissed him and then hurried away to wait on another customer. Buck noticed her long legs, highlighted by her short red velvet uniform dress that did little to cover her ruffled red panties. She soon returned with drinks for the two tables. Instead of the Coors Buck had ordered, she brought him a Wild Turkey and water. Though he started to say something, the protest never left his mouth. After drinking two strong bourbons, he sank back into the overstuffed chair.

Susie began sucking on his earlobe, Georgia also in the competition, massaging his left nipple with deft fingers while blowing hot air on the sensitive side of his neck. Trapped in an alcoholic haze, he felt as though he had died and gone to heaven. A tap on his shoulder broke the spell. It was Roy Dunlap and he was staring an angry hole directly through him. Georgia extricated herself, hugging and kissing the older man as he joined them at the table. His appearance resulted in the rapid departure of about half the people in the party. Soon, there was no one left except Ty, Susie, Roy, Georgia and Buck.

Buck ordered chicken livers and cream gravy, a house specialty, then excused himself to visit the little cowboy's room. When he returned, he found Ty had exchanged places with Susie and Roy Dunlap with Georgia. Just as well, he thought. He still needed to return home and feed the horses. When Ronnie arrived with yet another round of drinks, he pulled her toward him and whispered in her ear.

"Unless you intend to drive me home, I think you better replace this with a large hot coffee."

Buck knew Ronnie was married and only flirted with customers to enhance her tips. She understood his less than cryptic message. Taking his whiskey, she smiled and kissed him, soon returning with coffee and more drinks for the rest of the party. Buck realized Susie and Ty were an item, facing each other, knee-to-knee, engaged in a whispered but frenetic conversation. Roy Dunlap had his back to Buck, also engaged in a whispered conversation with Georgia.

She continued smiling at him, along with an occasional wink. Susie was pretty, but Georgia a classic beauty with Ingrid Bergman cheekbones and Marilyn Monroe eyes. Her short skirt had ridden up over her athletic thighs, either because of alcoholic indulgence, or more likely by design. He only had to wonder for a moment why she was attracted to the much older Dunlap before realizing it was a case of "checks appeal."

Suddenly locked out of the ensuing conversations, he asked Ronnie to bring him his tab.

"You're money's no good tonight. Roy's got it covered," she said, hurrying off to wait on another table.

"Gotta go," he finally said, standing to leave.

No one protested, but Georgia followed him to the door.

"You don't remember me but we have met."

Buck stared at her, dubious he had met such a gorgeous woman and forgotten about it. "Oh?" The only word he could muster.

"KK and I were roomies at OU. She introduced us in Norman one night, at a sorority party."

"That explains it," he said. "I went a while during my college years without sobering up. Still, I can't imagine forgetting you."

Georgia grinned. "See you tomorrow. I'll tell KK I

saw you," she said, warming his body when she pressed her bosom against his chest.

Reeling from the effects of the bourbon, he stumbled out the door to the covered parking lot where he found the black Lincoln Navigator Clayton had provided as his company car. The big SUV was new, the sales sticker still on the back window. He didn't have to read it to know the vehicle was expensive.

A myriad of thoughts crossed his mind as he drove down Northwest Expressway. Roy Dunlap is Clayton's best friend. He is married but has a mistress who is the best friend of Kay Karson, Buck's former girlfriend and who now appears to have something going with Clayton. A plethora of possible scenarios filled his brain as he steered the big Navigator toward Sunset Farms.

Chapter 5

The first thing Buck and Pard saw the next morning when they walked outside the barn was the black Lincoln. It seemed even larger in the sunlight. Buck grinned as he considered how he would retrieve his truck from the parking lot of the Petro Place. If nothing else, he could just leave it there until completing his job for Clayton. He had little knowledge about cattle rustling but knew someone that did. After finishing his morning chores, he gave him a call.

Buck had known Trey Calderham since high school. An investigator for the Texas and Southwestern Cattle Raisers Association, Calderham now carried a 9 mm Glock. As a special agent for both the Texas Department of Safety and the Oklahoma State Bureau of Investigation, he enjoyed full police powers in both Texas and Oklahoma and could legally arrest a cattle thief in either state if he caught one.

Trey was short, about five seven, and didn't look much like a lawman. The same age as Buck, he seemed older because of his prominent bald spot and the hint of gray in his moustache and otherwise brown hair. The leather jacket he usually wore concealed his pistol, but he liked to flash his silver badge.

Trey and Buck were friends but the two had tangled on many occasions while growing up. Despite his diminutive size, Trey could hold his own in a fight, a fact Buck had learned at an early age. The little man was Buck's closest friend.

Pard wasn't happy when Buck left him again with Hector, but Calderham asked to meet him at Stockman's Café near the stockyards in southwest Oklahoma City. A long line of people snaked down the sidewalk, waiting to get into the popular restaurant. Trey was near the head of the line and motioned Buck to join him.

"Stockman's is too damn popular, but it's the best restaurant in town, at least for my money."

"You keep your money. Treat's on me today."

Trey chuckled. "Mighty big of you, seeing as you need my help and all."

"I owe you one anyway since you drove me home from Pandora's last summer."

Trey grinned, remembering the hot July night when Buck, licking his wounds because of a lost love affair, had drank too many beers at Pandora's, a popular strip joint in Oklahoma City. At least he'd had the presence of mind to call Trey to come get him.

"You may just be more trouble than you are worth."

Buck didn't bother commenting as Wanda, a waitress who had worked at Stockman's for as long as he could remember, escorted them to a table in back of the large and noisy restaurant.

"Need I ask, or should I just bring your regular?"

Trey nodded. "Wanda, you know me too well."

"Better make it two," Buck said.

Trey rested his elbows on the table. "I didn't realize how well you are doing."

"Huh?"

"That decked out SUV you drove up in. You can't tell me you're making that kind of money."

It was Buck's turn to grin. "Who says?"

"If so, I'm ordering a ribeye."

"Order anything you like. I'm on an expense account and the Navigator is my company vehicle while I'm working on this case."

"Hell, maybe I should get a fifth of whiskey with my steak."

"I'll buy you two fifths if you let me watch you drink them."

"I'm tempted to take you up on it just to show you I could. Now what's so important?"

Buck explained Clayton's problem and finished by saying, "I don't understand why someone would risk stealing a few head of cattle."

"You checked the price of beef lately? A trailer load of cows can bring twenty grand. I'm pretty sure Clayton's cows are worth lots more."

"What'll we do?" Buck asked.

"We have inspectors working all the sale barns. They check brands, breeds, descriptions and ear tags, and send the information to our computer center in Fort Worth. If you have a description of the stolen cows, chances are we'll catch the thief."

"I have all the information on a computer database."

"Here's my email address," Trey said, handing Buck a business card. "Get me the info soon as possible. The sale of those steers may have already happened."

Wanda returned before they had a chance to finish their conversation. "Calf fries, compliments of me and the cook."

Trey put a fork into one of the delicacies and ate it. Calf fries, breaded and fried calf testicles were the specialty of the house. The dish often gave pause to new patrons of the restaurant.

"You're a doll, Wanda," he said. "When are you going to leave your old man and marry me?"

"You couldn't handle me," she said.

Buck grinned and shook his head as Wanda disappeared into the crowd. "Do you have a new squeeze since we last talked?"

Trey drummed the side of his plate with his fork as if he had something gnawing on his insides. He finally looked Buck in the eye.

"Guess I'm gonna have to tell you sometime," he said. "Beth O'Hara and I are a couple now. We both hope you understand."

Trey's admission caught Buck by surprise. Buck and Beth, owner of the Azure Pendant, a restaurant in Oklahoma City's Paseo District, had been a number for almost a year. Circumstances had ended their relationship and Buck was surprised either Beth or Trey would care what his thoughts were.

"I'm happy for both of you. I loved her dearly but our relationship was over long ago. I can't think of anyone I would more like her to connect with."

"Thanks. I been meaning to tell you for weeks now, and you don't know how much this means to me you understand the situation."

Buck had met Beth while on an investigation of a Cherokee artist who had met his demise at the hands of his own ex-wife. Ten years older, she fostered a persona lodged somewhere between hippy flower child and American Indian maiden. Her tousled thatch of red hair and peaches and cream complexion belied anything except Irish descent. She had a penchant for squash blossom necklaces, dream catchers and American Indian art. She was also an excellent chef specializing in southwestern cuisine. Despite their age disparity, they had enjoyed a good time line-dancing, horseback riding and making passionate afternoon love. Only Buck's roaming proclivities had caused the demise of the relationship. Now, he couldn't even remember the other woman's name.

"Who are you dating now? Maybe we can all go to dinner next week."

"Just playing the field for the last few months."

"Uh huh. I've never known you not to have two or three women on the line at any given time."

"Being broke plays hell on your love life."

"Uh huh," Trey said again.

They continued their friendly banter as they ate. Buck finally turned the conversation back to the problem at hand.

"Clayton seems to think one of his hands might be involved. At least providing information to the actual thief."

Trey nodded. "Not so far fetched. We see it all the time."

"He also suspects people living in a commune surrounded by his ranch. Know anything about it?"

Trey shook his head, but Wanda had overheard Buck's question.

"Pagan lesbians. Mostly women who finally worked up the nerve to leave their old men."

"Glad you are checking them out and not me. Hey, I hate to eat and run but I have an appointment in Piedmont at three."

"You've helped me a lot. How do you know so much about Clayton's cows?"

"He has one of the highest quality Black Angus herds in the state. His and Roy Dunlap's are tops."

"Interesting? Where is Dunlap's ranch?"

"North of Guthrie. Almost as big and fancy as Mr. O'Meara's."

Buck pondered the possible implications of Roy Dunlap's ranch ownership as he waited outside the restaurant while Trey visited the men's room. He soon joined him, a cell phone to his ear.

"That was Beth. How about dinner at our house?"

"You two live together?"

"I'll send you the address when I acknowledge your email. Don't beg off on me or you'll miss one of the best home-cooked meals you've ever had."

"Count me in," Buck said.

Trey waved and tooled away in his red Jeep Wrangler. As Buck walked past the line of people still extending out of the restaurant, he worried about the impending dinner engagement, wondering just how awkward it would be.

Chapter 6

Buck learned, upon returning to Sunset Farms Hector had taken to Pard, and vice versa.

"I hope he's not bothering you."

"You kidding? He's more help than another hand. Smartest dog I ever seen and he handles the horses better than me."

"I sensed a little separation anxiety when I left this morning."

Pard was happy to see him but didn't protest being left behind with Hector again later the same day. When Buck pulled up to the 2nd Bank of Edmond in the new Navigator, the first person he saw was his little loan officer. Jeb Stuart Johnson's moustache twitched as he watched Buck exit the luxury Lincoln.

"You get a loan from another bank?" he asked before saying hi.

"Company car," Buck said. "I'm on the payroll at Crescent Oil."

"Well then maybe now I can give you the truck loan."

"I'm just here to make a deposit."

As Buck waited at the teller's window, he realized even after catching up on his overdue bills, he had almost enough money in his account to make a down payment on a new truck. He didn't need one now. When he did, he'd already decided to take his business somewhere else. His banking finished, he pointed the Navigator toward Clayton's ranch. His conversation with Trey had spawned some questions only the wealthy oil man could answer.

Snow began falling as he drove through the open gate to Clayton's ranch. When he pulled up to the back porch, he noticed the two-seater Mercedes he was sure was KK's. He hadn't yet confronted her about her relationship with Clayton. After their meeting at the Edmond coffee shop, he realized he probably needed to. Clayton waited in the veranda's door, a glass of whiskey in his hand.

"Bout time you got here." He motioned for Buck to join him in the porch swing draped with the colorful serape. "I guess by now you heard about me and KK."

"I got no problem with it. Whatever she and I had ended long ago."

"I appreciate that."

The edge in Clayton's voice disappeared. Finishing his whiskey, he signaled Maria for another. Snowfall was picking up outside the veranda as his harried assistant brought his fresh drink.

"I had a meeting with a friend of mine that works for the Texas and Southwestern Cattle Raisers Association. I asked him to help me in the investigation. I hope its okay with you."

"Sounds like you are making progress," Clayton said after sipping his whiskey. "Right now, I want you to visit the compound and find out for me what's going on over there."

Buck opened his mouth but words didn't spring forth. His first month's salary still warm in his bank account, he realized whatever Clayton wanted, he also wanted.

"Okay, Boss, I'll check it out."

Clayton nodded, already knowing the power of his money. "Try to buy the property from them if you can."

"I'll do my best."

"I know you will," Clayton said, grinning. "Taking care of that little matter might work out nicely right about now, but you go when you feel like it."

It didn't take Buck long to realize Clayton's wishes were his orders. He exited the veranda with a smile and a snappy salute. It continued snowing as he returned to his car and saw someone he recognized. KK tried to ignore him but he was having none of it.

"Why are you treating me like this?" he demanded. "I've never done anything to hurt you."

"I really like Clayton and don't need you messing things up for me."

"Is that what this is all about?"

"I like you a lot, Buck McDivit, but Clayton is different."

Snowflakes fell on his shoulders as he grabbed her arms. "Whatever we once had is over. I liked you as much as any woman I've ever known but I've moved on now."

KK's expression changed and she hugged him. "You know I'll always love you but I've also moved on. Clayton's now the love of my life."

"And I promise I won't do anything to change things."

"I'm so sorry," she said. "Georgia told me you are doing some work for Clayton at his oil company. I was already paranoid after what happened with her and me, and I just got a little skitsy."

"About what?"

She tugged on his hand, motioning him to sit with her in the front seat of her Mercedes.

"In case you haven't already figured it out, Georgia is Roy Dunlap's girlfriend. I hung out with them a lot until they introduced me to Clayton. One night, I went with them to a dog fight."

"You like dog fights?"

"Not me, Roy. I think it's repulsive and so does Georgia."

"But you went anyway?"

KK nodded. "Roy's a real freak. He not only owns fighting dogs and roosters, he bets thousands on them. I can't begin to tell you all the crazy things he's into."

"Such as?"

"He has an animal farm. You know what I mean?" Buck shook his head. "He owns a place in rural Logan County where rich spectators pay to see prostitutes have sex with animals."

"You gotta be kidding."

"I'm not, and the person who runs it for him is a man named Jimmy Quick. He does lots of other things for Roy."

"Such as?"

"You name it. He's a gorgeous man and so vain he wears a necklace with a diamond-encrusted letter Q pendant. Georgia and I decided to look him up one night when Roy and Clayton were out of town. We ended up taking him to Georgia's house."

"And now you're afraid he'll tell Roy and Clayton."

"I don't think so because Roy pays him lots of money, but Georgia and I got scared when we went to one of the dog fights."

"What happened?"

"Jimmy carries a big knife and cut his dog's throat with it when he lost a big fight. Buck, please don't tell any of this to Clayton. I don't think he knows how warped Roy is and I don't want him finding out because of me."

***

Early March snow had increased and Buck put the Navigator into four-wheel-drive as he followed the slippery section line road to the entrance of the commune. Skeleton Creek split Clayton's large ranch. The commune lay on the north side of his property and was oddly shaped because of the meandering course of the large creek. Buck followed a road, paved with gravel by some rich oil company. After passing a pumping well, he continued along a less improved road until he reached a barren grove of trees shrouding the pathway with leafless winter limbs. Around the bend, Buck got a big surprise. The sight he encountered was unlike anything he had expected.

There was something different about the hillside north of the bluffs and it took him a moment to realize what it was. Falling snow lessened and the scene came into focus. Dome-shaped structures protruding from the ground were actually buildings, most the size of houses, some even larger.

Partially sunk into the ground, the buildings seemed eerily abnormal beneath their coating of snow. Before Buck had time to reflect on the scene, a small jeep-like vehicle enclosed by a canvas top pulled up beside him. Two women, both dressed in uniforms identifying them as cops, exited the vehicle.

"Can we help you?" The older of the two women asked when he rolled down his window.

"Your neighbor, Clayton O'Meara wants to make an offer on this property and he sent me to see if you were interested."

The two women exchanged glances, as if they had expected him. "Come with us," one of them said.

Leaving the Navigator unlocked, he climbed into the rear seat of the strange vehicle. The two women could pass as mother and daughter. Both had dark eyes and hair pulled back into severe buns. Neither had visible weapons but their demeanors left little doubt they could maintain or restore order. Glancing out the window, he wondered how much snow would accumulate before morning.

There was no engine noise, only the silent whirr of what he guessed was an electric motor. Falling snow had washed all the color from the terrain, the vehicle's silence meshing with diminished tactile and aural sensations of the scenery around them.

The women drove the electric vehicle a short distance to the largest visible dome-shaped building where they exited, motioning Buck to follow. They led him through the heavy oak doors of the building where a bustle of noisy activity replaced outside silence.

A dozen women were at work, mostly with computers. Ambient light from well-placed ceiling windows filled the room. Buck could see no light bulbs or fluorescent lighting, only the strange but effective glow from panels similar to those found in computer screens. All activity in the room ceased as Buck followed the two women down a hallway to a closed door guarded by a secretary sitting behind her desk.

"We have a messenger from O'Meara."

The young woman glanced at Buck, stood from her chair and knocked on the door. She opened it just enough to enter, shutting it behind her.

Buck waited for the two cops. Instead, they exited in the direction they had come. The young blonde woman held the door open for him.

"Can I get you something to drink?"

She nodded and smiled when he said, "Coffee, black, please."

An attractive woman standing behind a lectern greeted him.

"I am Lana, chief administrator of Lykaia. How can I be of service?"

Lana was tall, every inch the match of Buck's six feet, long red hair draping her shoulders. A squash blossom necklace emphasizing turquoise and native silver hung from her regal neck, extending into the plunging neckline of the azure dress matching her eyes. Similar bracelets encircled both her wrists. Her expressive eyes, pouting lips, and figure that would have well served a super model accented a beautiful face that could launch a thousand dreams. Buck caught his breath before he spoke.

"I'm Buck McDivit. Clayton O'Meara sent me to see if you would consider an offer for your property."

Lana smiled. "If that's all you want, I'm afraid you're wasting your time. This is our home and we don't intend to leave it."

"Can't we even talk about it?"

"Talk is cheap, Mr. McDivit."

"I've never seen anything like this place. Is there a chance someone might show me around?"

"For what reason?"

"I'll need something to tell Mr. O'Meara, why you can't bear to leave for any price."

"Maybe Mr. O'Meara should come see for himself. Meantime, I will personally give you a tour."

She didn't bother turning out the lights. As if by magic, the room darkened when his beautiful tour guide opened the door. They spent time touring the business complex, and then looking at a detailed map, Lana pointing out landmarks and explaining a bit about the commune. It was already growing dark when she led him down an elaborate tunnel system lighted by the same peculiar glow as in her office.

They soon reached another building, its interior dim and atmospheric. Patrons occupied seats around cozy tables. By the aroma wafting from the rear door, he pegged the place as a restaurant. Without waiting for someone to direct them, Lana strolled to a table on a raised terrace and motioned him to join her.

"The Tiers is one of three restaurants we have here in Lykaia, this one so-called because of its terraced arrangement."

"Lykaia is a beautiful name."

"Inspired by an ancient Greek festival."

Wonderful music emerging from somewhere in the dark room soon transformed Buck's thoughts to other things. When his eyes adjusted to the dimness, he realized the music was live, coming from a string quartet on a small stage. A young woman approached.

She asked, "Will you be dining with us tonight?"

Lana glanced at Buck. "Have you eaten? If you have, we can just have drinks while we talk."

"The aroma coming from the kitchen is wonderful." Lana smiled and told the waitperson they would be eating. "I'll have whatever you're having," he said.

"This is not a normal restaurant, Mr. McDivit. The menu tonight will be what everyone here eats. We grow much of our own produce and what we don't cultivate ourselves, we trade for with neighboring farmers."

"The lighting is unusual," Buck said.

"Light emitting diodes. We burn no fossil fuels and generate electricity with a combination of solar and wind power, both of which are abundant in Oklahoma."

"The vehicle in which your officers brought me here is electric."

"We also use animal and human waste to create fuel. We make our own fuels from various plants, but just enough for our own needs."

"Your houses are passive solar."

"We partially bury our dome homes and buildings to harness the earth's natural heating and cooling properties. They all face south and we gather the sun's energy in the winter and use reflectors to divert it in the summer. We bury our heat pumps so their temperature remains constant, no matter what the season."

"And the tunnel system?"

"Tunnels connect all the buildings. This is for protection from the elements, safety and convenience. Dome homes are very secure and especially safe from tornadoes and other weather phenomena quite common here in Oklahoma."

"How do your people support themselves?"

"We are doctors, lawyers, writers, artists and musicians. We all have our talents. I have an MBA from OU, which is why I am in administration. We all contribute our skills for the common good."

"You don't use money?"

"Not in Lykaia, but we don't all live here. Many of our people hold jobs in towns throughout the State. We have pooled our resources. That's how we purchased this land and paid for most of the construction. Still, we do as much bartering as we can and have alliances with other groups throughout the country, the world, and with companies and individuals we can mutually assist."

"I see," Buck said as the young woman returned with their dinner.

Expecting some vegetarian fare, ala Trey's description, he was quite delighted instead by baked tilapia, green beans and a pilaf of rice. There was also a chilled bottle of white wine. The waitperson popped the cork and then handed it to Buck for his acceptance. Following a sip, his nod and broad smile, she poured a glass for Lana, and then topped his.

"You look surprised."

"I don't know why, but I expected everyone here to be tee totaling vegetarians."

It was Lana's turn to smile. "We love our vegetables but most of us also eat meat. We raise tilapia here."

"Even in the winter?"

"In underground ponds, Mr. McDivit. That is the key."

"Wonderful. Your wine is very good."

"Our very own Skeleton Creek Chardonnay."

"You have a winery?"

"Oh yes. We produced our first cask last year. We have several varietals we are cultivating. The grapes grow on the slopes above the creek."

Buck gazed into Lana's eyes, suddenly intoxicated by her beauty and the wonderful wine. "You have no men."

"You noticed," Lana said with a smile. "Our commune is only for females."

"Are you . . . ?"

"Lesbians?"

Buck grinned. "It's really none of my business."

"We are much like a microcosm of the population of the world. Some of our members are lesbians and some are very much heterosexual. We are all here for the common good, but mostly because of our beliefs. Every citizen of Lykaia practices the same religion, Mr. McDivit. Some people call us pagans." Buck's mouth opened wide but no words came out. Blinking once, he just smiled and shook his head.

She stared at him and said, "No comment?"

"Except for weddings and funerals, I haven't been to church in fifteen years. At least you believe in something."

Lana seemed satisfied with his answer. Smiling, she sipped her wine before asking another question.

"What about you, Mr. McDivit? You have a smooth way of eliciting information. What exactly is your line of work?"

"I was a cop for a while, and then I tried my hand as an oil and gas lease broker when the oil companies began paying so well. I've done a little bounty hunting, acted as an assistant death examiner, worked from time to time for the Logan County Sheriff, and have even ridden in a few professional rodeos. I think of myself as a private investigator."

"And now you work for Mr. O'Meara?"

"For the moment," Buck said, his answer sounding a little defensive.

"Would you consider doing a job for me?"

"What do you have in mind?"

Lana tapped her fork against the table, not immediately answering his question. The string quartet continued playing in the background, Buck suddenly aware it was an old Beatle's tune.

"An outsider is harassing us. Our police protect us, but I need someone to find out who it is and determine their motivation—someone who has a good working relationship with the Logan County Sheriff's Department in the event we need to press charges. You might fit the picture."

"I have a conflict since I'm working for Mr. O'Meara."

"We all have conflicts, Mr. McDivit. From what I can sense, you have enough integrity to overcome any possible conflict that might exist."

"I would have to clear it with my boss."

Lana smiled and said, "I wouldn't have it any other way."

The meal finished and the string quartet on a break, the only sound remaining was the slight hum of electric fans controlling airflow as they left the restaurant.

"Can you return to Lykaia for a briefing?"

"I can, day after tomorrow."

"Perfect. When you return, bring a change of clothes and plan to spend two days with us. I'll explain later."

Lana's words left him with more questions than answers. The last time a beautiful female had told him she would explain something later, he'd lost a week's wages and gained a pain which resided in his heart for almost a year.

***

It was well after dark when the two female police officers returned him to his Navigator. Snow covered the first third of the SUV's eighteen-inch wheels but someone had cleaned his windshield of ice and snow. He didn't bother returning to Clayton's ranch, heading instead to his own place at Sunset Farms.

He strolled through the barn, checking all the horses along with his own pony Lady. They were all watered, fed and seemed happy and settled in for the night. Pard joined him, excited he had finally returned. As they climbed the stairs to the luxury suite, he vowed to buy Hector Ramirez a bottle of whiskey.

Buck's apartment was on the second floor of the barn, along with a half dozen other rooms, vacant now and used mostly by visiting jockeys racing at local Remington Park. His suite was finished in rare woods, granite and the finest silk. It always made him feel as if he were staying in a luxury hotel in some exotic part of the world. A message from Trey Calderham was on his answering machine.

"Did you forget your cell phone? Call me when you get in. I have some information for you."

Buck glanced at his twenty-year-old Rolex. After ten, it was too late to return Trey's message. He would call first thing in the morning. Right now, he was dog-tired and needed a few quality hours of sleep. Ten minutes after hitting the expensive Swedish mattress, he was already in dreamland.

Chapter 7

Buck awoke the following morning with Pard licking his face. Fraught with too much information to process and not enough time to accomplish the task, his sleep had been fitful. Shaking off his unanswered questions, he washed his face in the marble-topped bathroom sink and then went downstairs with Pard to feed the horses.

Stirring, they awaited his caresses and gentle words. He didn't disappoint. The barn was a modern piece of architectural design constructed by Amish artisans Clayton had flown in from Pennsylvania and paid handsomely for their efforts. They had painstakingly thought out every minute detail, including an escape route in the event of fire. Hector Ramirez liked to refer to the barn as the eighth wonder of the world.

Buck's own pony, Lady was an Oklahoma Paint horse. High-spirited, she didn't like it when he failed to ride her, even for one day. Knowing as much, he patted her neck, calming her as she voiced her displeasure for not having seen him in two days. Throwing a blanket and saddle on her back, he cinched the strap and led her out of the stall toward the open door of the barn.

Morning Mist of Blood

Snow still covered the ground and warm breath swirled from Lady's nostrils as she started toward the road in rapt anticipation. Buck was up for the ride, having missed her as much as she had missed him. When they reached the snow-cleared County road, Pard racing behind them, he slapped her rear, propelling her forward at a breakneck clip. A half mile later, he reined in the panting pony, stretching his arms around her big neck.

"Lady, you are the only female who has ever understood me." When she whinnied and tapped her foot on the road, he added, "Maybe too well."

Buck had purposely left his cell phone in his room. When he returned, he had two missed messages, one from Trey, the other from Clayton. He wanted to jump in the shower and luxuriate beneath warm water until he felt totally revived. Instead, he dialed Trey.

"What's up?"

"Three cows turned up at a local auction yesterday. Two were Black Angus, the third a breed no one recognized. Our agents identified them as belonging to Mr. O'Meara. There was no ear tag or lip tattoo on the strange cow and it was too young for a brand."

"Then how could they tell it was one of Clayton's?"

"Some of our agents have judged cattle competitions at state fairs and such. They could see this cow, even though they couldn't identify the breed, was show quality and it got them to thinking something might be wrong."

"And?"

"They took blood sample for analysis. The DNA report on the two Black Anguses confirmed they were from Clayton's herd. It's just reasonable the third was also one of Mr. O'Meara's."

"Who was the seller?"

"A loser named Johnny Crabtree."

"Did they arrest him?"

"There are bigger fish to fry here. I'm emailing you

the details, and don't forget about dinner tonight."

"I'll be there," Buck said before hanging up the phone, hoping Trey didn't hear the insincerity in his voice.

Buck owed Clayton a call but decided his shower couldn't wait. Stripping down, he stepped beneath cascading water in Mrs. O'Meara's world-class shower, finished in Italian marble and big enough for half a dozen good friends. Like the fantasy worlds of many young men, his always grew larger in the shower. Today, as warm water splayed over his naked body, he could hardly keep his imagination from concocting fantasies about the beautiful Lana and her long red hair. Maybe she wanted him to spend the night so he could satisfy her own fantasy about him. As water streamed cold in the shower, he realized it was probably not the case.

Like water in the hot and steamy shower, his fantasy cooled. The daydream, no matter how improbable, was imprudent because, technically, he was now her employee, assuming Clayton didn't protest. He plopped down into an overstuffed chair, so comfortable he had trouble getting out of it whenever he sat in it. Finally dragging away from its grasp, he called Clayton.

"Tell me about your visit to the commune."

"There are a couple hundred people there and they have all combined their assets. I'd say they are more able to buy you out than vice versa."

There was silence on the phone for a long moment before Clayton finally said, "That's not what I wanted to hear."

"Don't shoot me, I'm only the messenger."

Clayton thought for a moment before saying, "Information is power. I want you to go back and get as much as possible.

"No problem. They want to hire me to do some investigative work for them. I thought I better pass it by you before I accepted."

"Sounds like a perfect opportunity to spy on them for me."

"I don't spy on people I'm working for," Buck said

"Don't get your panties in a wad," Clayton said, "I wasn't suggesting you stab anyone in the back."

"They seem willing to tell me everything I want to know, and Lana, the person who runs the place, issued you an invitation to check out things for yourself."

"Oh yeah?"

"You ought to go just to see her. A real looker."

"What else?"

"Have you heard of a man named Johnny Crabtree?"

"Worked here on the ranch a time or two, but just part time. Look, Buck, I have to go now. We'll talk about this later," Clayton said, hanging up the phone.

"Damn it!" Buck muttered under his breath. "Working for that man is like beating yourself in the head with a ball peen hammer."

Chores completed and feeling considerably better, he said goodbye to Pard and headed for town. He'd decided to spend the day reading every entry in the computer database until he had a better picture of Clayton's cattle operation. He didn't know what he would accomplish by revisiting Lykaia, but he looked forward to seeing gorgeous Lana again. Pretty Susie met him at the front door.

"We missed you last night."

"Hey, I missed you too, but I was working."

She grinned and asked, "Anybody I know?"

On impulse, he bent her over and kissed her full on the mouth. Susie's green eyes grew big and she said, "Whoa, cowboy, you're starting to give me ideas."

"I already have a few about you," he replied, heading down the hall to his office. Shutting the door behind him, he pulled up the database of Clayton's cattle operation, soon finding what he was looking for.

Clayton's foreman, Garth Dunlap was the man responsible for periodically hiring Johnny Crabtree.

"Dunlap?" Buck said as someone opened his door.

"Yes?"

Buck glanced up to see buttoned-down Roy Dunlap. "Do you know a man named Garth Dunlap?"

"My little brother, a perennial ne'er-do-well. Clayton was kind enough to give him a job."

Dunlap nodded when Buck said, "Clayton's foreman?"

"What's he done now?"

"Nothing, I was just reading Clayton's employee list and wondered if you two are related."

"Garth was a change of life baby for my parents. I had already graduated high school when he was born. We were never close."

Buck glanced out the big picture window at traffic streaming past on Northwest Expressway, not wanting Roy Dunlap to know how interested he really was in his younger brother. When Dunlap left his office, he continued scanning files, stopping only briefly to order lunch from Nick's, working as he ate. It was five when he finally glanced at his watch.

Turning off the laptop, he thought about his impending dinner date with Trey and former girlfriend Beth O'Hara. He hadn't seen her since their breakup and had only talked to her once on the phone. She had made several, probably very true but still uncomplimentary remarks about him and they continued to plague his memory of her.

He wasn't looking forward to seeing Miss O'Hara but he didn't want to hurt Trey's feelings. His thoughts drifted to his short time with Beth as he pointed the Navigator toward the Paseo, Oklahoma City's old art district. She had a restaurant, the Azure Pendant, where they first met.

***

Although not far from the Petro Place, The Paseo

District occupied a much older part of town. A big Oklahoma sky had grown dark as Buck cruised through the cemetery north of the Paseo and entered the little art district. A diamond in the rough, the area waited patiently for the next real estate boom. It reminded him of Santa Fe with its stucco buildings painted pink and garish blue. There were a couple of restaurants, a few nightclubs, a head shop, several art studios and little else. Beth's restaurant and club was the most popular establishment in the Paseo.

Her manager was running the place tonight, something which never happened when he was dating her. Stymied by her workaholic tendencies, he'd often found himself wishing during their brief relationship the restaurant would catch fire and burn to the ground.

When he dated Beth, she lived in the second story of a tiny apartment in a complex located west of the restaurant. Trey had somehow convinced her to move to new digs, although still located in the Paseo. He had purchased a two-story building, once the office of a group of eclectic architects. Buck looked forward to inspecting it, even as he rued his meeting with her.

When he first met Beth, she seemed everything he ever wanted in a woman. Later, he realized she was probably everything he ever needed in a mother. The thought confounded him, and left their relationship in shambles. Parking on the street beside Trey's flame red Jeep Wrangler, he strolled to the door.

"Come on in this place, Cowboy," Trey said, opening the blonde oak and cut glass door almost before Buck had time to ring the bell.

The new abode was everything Buck had imagined and more. Trey led him through an entryway, to a living area painted in earth tones and decorated with American Indian art. In addition to the paintings, antique Indian blankets graced the walls.

"We could have bought a Mercedes for what I paid for that one," Trey said, pointing at an Indian blanket mounted like a piece of art.

"It's quite old and worth every penny," a feminine voice said from behind.

It was Beth, dressed much the same as the first time Buck had met her, in a faux-buckskin dress and an azure feather in her raven-red hair. She was smiling so he hugged her.

At least ten years older, she was one of those lucky people who never seemed to age. Not beautiful in the classic sense, she exuded sex. He held on to her for a moment too long, his hands remembering the softness and warmth of her shoulders, her red hair reminding him of Lana.

"Ahem," Trey said, clearing his throat.

"Sorry," Buck said, pulling away from her. "Guess I had forgotten just how gorgeous Beth is. I never could keep my hands off her. You are a lucky man Trey."

"I'm the lucky one," Beth said, giving Buck a chance to wipe the silly grin off his face. "Trey's the best man I ever met."

"Ouch!" Buck said.

"That's why I love her," Trey said. "Let us show you the rest of the place."

Once a large open studio, Trey and Beth had converted the space into a gorgeous apartment. The two-storied building had a wonderful view from its large open balcony overlooking the Paseo. Trey and Buck relaxed on a sofa draped with a bright red Navajo rug, and Beth brought them cold mugs of beer.

"You two have things to talk about," she said. "I'll be in the kitchen and will let you know when dinner is ready."

"Great view and so relaxing," Buck said. "If I lived here, I'd never get anything done.

Trey sipped his beer and nodded. "She likes you a lot."

"I like her. Good thing for you we broke up."

Trey smiled. "She is a dream woman."

By now, the effects of the second beer were acting on Buck. "Is this a strong brew I'm drinking?"

Trey's smile grew larger. "I visit Fort Worth every week or so and always return with a case or two.

Oklahoma has strange liquor laws resulting in big beer companies refusing to sell anything but three-point-two beer in the state. The beer Buck was drinking had considerably more alcohol and he felt his cheeks grow progressively warmer.

"Something bothers me. What makes Clayton's cows so unique?"

"How much do you know about cattle?"

Trey chuckled when Buck answered, "T-bone, medium rare."

"There are maybe eight hundred breeds of cattle divided roughly between cold and hot climate varieties. Ranchers want a breed that has few calving problems and consistently produces quality beef. There are around fifty common cattle breeds in the United States."

"Like Black Angus?"

"Oklahoma is an unusual state weather wise. A valuable breed is one which can survive our cold winters, hot summers and still have consistent qualities."

"You think Clayton has developed such a breed?"

"That's the rumor on the street. Clayton's cows supposedly thrive in Oklahoma and have the qualities our breeder's desire. The cow Crabtree sold in the auction might qualify as a new breed."

"How would you know?"

"I guess we'd have to see a bunch of cows with similar traits."

"What is something like developing a new breed worth?"

"I can't count that high but to make the finances work, the breeder has to control access to his stock. Other breeders pay license fees for the right to raise the cattle and form associations to protect their rights."

"You know something else, don't you?"

Trey grinned. "The DNA sample we took of the unusual cow Crabtree sold indicates it's a variety of cattle none of us has ever seen before."

Buck had to think a moment about the implications of what Trey had just told him."If someone stole a truckload of cows, why did they only try to sell three of them?"

"Don't know for sure but I have a theory."

"Which is?"

"Say three men were hired to perform the actual theft. Maybe they stole an extra three cows to sell and split the proceeds, not telling the person that hired them. The three extras they took were Black Angus but they wouldn't all fit in their stock trailer. In the confusion, they probably shooed away an Angus. Being short, they sold one of the special breed instead at the auction."

"Then you think the cattle thieves were working for someone else."

Trey nodded. "Someone who badly wanted a sampling of Clayton's new breed."

People were milling on the street below, moving slowly between clubs. Music wafted up from the nightspots, filling the early spring night with sounds of jazz and salsa music. The temperature was in the fifties, much milder than the previous day when snow covered the ground. Mostly melted now, there was still a nip of winter in the air, but not enough to keep Trey and Buck, and the revelers below from enjoying a wonderful late March evening.

"Tell me about Johnny Crabtree," Buck finally said.

"A real piece of work. He lives in a trailer house northwest of Crescent in a little community of like-minded people."

"Oh?"

"Redneck racists with larceny in their veins, linked to everything from home invasions to crystal meth, and probably everything in between."

"So Crabtree had two partners."

"Yes, and all three were working for someone else. Someone smarter than Crabtree. You can bet good money on it.

Sticking her head out the door, Beth interrupted their discussion. "If you boys can quit yakking for a while, dinner is ready."

They followed her inside, Buck's senses aroused by the aroma drifting from the kitchen. Beth seated them at a table in a cozy nook and then began serving dinner. As Buck savored his first bite, he remembered one of the reasons he liked her so much.

"This is wonderful."

"Roast pork loin with red chile peanut molé. It's my variation of a recipe I picked up in New Mexico."

Trey and Beth laughed when Buck said "I might just have to fistfight you for Beth before the night's over."

When their laughter abated, she said, "Trey tells me you visited Lykaia, the Southern Death Cult Commune."

Buck did a double take "I don't have a clue what you mean by the Southern Death Cult."

"One of the oldest Native American sites in the U.S. is the Spiro Mounds in southeastern Oklahoma. The Mounds were a spiritual complex for the Southern Death Cult, a Native American religion. The Lykaians practice a modern form of this very old religion."

"You just told me something I didn't know," Trey said.

"I thought you were an expert on everything about Oklahoma."

"Maybe when it comes to cows. How do you know so much about the compound?"

"Their bank lent me the money to buy the Azure

Pendant."

"They have a bank?"

"Yes, but they only lend to, well, women."

"How did you find out about it?"

"You boys never have trouble getting anything you need, at least when it comes to business. It's not as easy for a woman, but word gets around."

"Are they lesbians?" Trey asked.

"Why would you even ask that question? Women live longer than men, not to mention husbands often leave their wives for someone younger. The group looks out for each other when there's not a man around to satisfy the role."

Trey gave her a sad puppy look. "That's not the way you feel about me, is it?"

"You're the best man I have ever known—far better than my creep first husband or the dreamy-eyed Casanova without a brain in his head who left me stranded after I followed him here from Texas. You know I love you."

"I guess I know now how you felt about me," Buck said with a grin, trying to impart a little levity back into the conversation.

It worked because Beth laughed and Trey guffawed, almost choking on his beer. "You know what I mean. Women sometimes need other women. Just like you two need each other from time to time."

Talk of the compound erased the smile from Trey's face and he began eating his red chile peanut molé.

"This is wonderful and your exes really were brainless."

It was true Beth could cook like no other, but it wasn't the most important quality Buck had liked about her. Nor was it sex, although she left him with no complaints in that particular category. She had an opinion on most everything, one she had thought out and not just thought up. Buck missed calling her for advice and hearing her opinions. Halfway through the molé, he realized he was only a disappearing blip on her radar screen.

***

It was late when he made it home to Sunset Farms but Hector was awake, whittling a hunk of wood as he sat on the porch of his house. Pard was with him and licked Buck's face when he joined them on the steps.

"You're up late. What's going on?"

"I stayed up to tell you a man dropped by tonight."

"What did he want?"

"You."

Hector was not an impulsive man. Something had spooked him.

"He asked how long I had known you and what you do for a living. I didn't know if he was a bill collector or what, so I didn't tell him much. Just enough to get him to leave."

"Did he say his name?"

"He said I didn't need to know who he was."

"What did he look like."

"A big man, six four or so, dressed in expensive jeans and boots. He wore lots of jewelry, a fancy watch, rings and a heavy gold necklace with a dangling letter."

"What letter?"

Hector had a stick in his hand and used it to trace the letter Q in the dirt in front of them.

Chapter 8

The late night visit by the mysterious man worried Buck as much as it had spooked Hector and LaDona, so he contacted his employer, Virginia O'Meara. An intensely private person, she immediately hired a local security firm to patrol the premises on a regular basis.

Following his talk with Trey, he had new questions for Clayton. The day seemed like spring, the sky blue and sunny as he headed toward Clayton's ranch. Pard wanted to come along but seemed to understand when Buck told him he needed to guard LaDona and the baby. Since Clayton wasn't expecting him, the guards detained him at the gate, harassing him unmercifully, as usual. It didn't matter because a call to the boss got the doors opened for him.

Buck parked outside the veranda and entered through the back door without knocking. He found a smiling Clayton sitting in his rocking chair, a ubiquitous glass of whiskey in his hand.

"You're up mighty early today."

It was Buck's turn to grin. "It's you who likes to sleep until eight every morning."

"Only when I got a good reason," Clayton said, glancing at his bedroom curtains.

"More power to you. KK was too much woman for me."

"You're really not mad at me because of her, are you?"

"We broke up long ago. I'm happy she landed with someone as stable as you are, and you're lucky because she's one hot woman."

"You don't have any doubts I can handle her, do you?"

Buck grinned again. "If you can, then you're a better man than I am." Outside, Clayton's cowboys were hurrying about as if something important had happened. "What's up?"

"Nothing really," Clayton answered.

There was a tacit hint in Clayton's abbreviated explanation which told Buck he was covering something up. "Come on, we're on the same side here."

All signs of Clayton's smile had disappeared. "We had another little robbery last night."

"And you were going to keep it from me?"

Clayton squirmed in his rocker. "There are things about my cattle operation we haven't discussed."

"Like your secret breed you didn't bother telling me about?"

Clayton glanced around the veranda to see if anyone was listening to the conversation.

"How do you know about that?"

"Trey told me."

Clayton motioned for Buck to follow him into the house.

"Walls have ears. There are certain things I only discuss in the privacy of my office.

The ranch house was huge and expensively decorated. Buck followed him down a teak-floored hallway, its walls lined with expensive paintings of different cattle breeds. Clayton finally stopped at a closed door equipped with a combination lock below the knob. Standing in front of the lock so neither Buck nor anyone else could see, he worked the combination and opened the door.

Clayton led him into a large room with no windows, motioning him to sit in an overstuffed leather chair while he locked the door behind them. He plopped down in a huge leather chair behind the largest desk Buck had ever seen, its woodwork so intricate it likely cost a small fortune. Gazing around the room, he took in the paraphernalia Clayton had probably spent a lifetime collecting.

Like the paintings in the hallway, cattle pictures occupied much of the wall space. There were also pictures of Clayton with many former presidents—both of the Bush's, and a smiling, much younger Clayton with his arm around Ronald Reagan. There was no sound from outside the room.

"This office is secure. The only place on this ranch that is. We can talk straight here. Want something to drink?"

"Coffee sounds good."

Clayton made a face before punching a button on his desk phone. "Maria, bring us some coffee." Without waiting for an answer, he replaced the receiver. Leaning on his elbows as he clasped his hands, he said, "Now tell me what you know about my cattle operation."

"Trey's people took DNA from a cow they were suspicious of at a sale barn. One of your cows. It wasn't a breed they were familiar with. Trey thinks you may be developing a new breed. Is it true?"

"Damn it! I've spent a million bucks trying to keep my operation quiet. Now everyone in central Oklahoma knows what I'm up to."

"Someone seems to know all about your new breed, and it may be the very reason you are losing cows. You need to tell me so we'll be on the same page."

Clayton took a healthy slug of his whiskey before answering. "My cows are bred specifically for

Oklahoma and Texas. The best cow ever produced for this region."

"What's something like that worth?"

"Ten times more than I ever made in the oil business."

"Then your secret is damn sure worth stealing. Did you know Roy Dunlap is into dog and chicken fighting?"

"What he does on his own time is his business."

"Maybe it's not as pretty as you think. Some of the things he's into stink to high heaven. A man named Jimmy Quick does most of his dirty work."

"What's this got to do with my cows?"

"Mr. Quick paid a visit to Sunset Farms last night, asking Hector and LaDona lots of questions about my background, and my relationship with you. Does Roy Dunlap know about your secret breed?"

"I've discussed it with him. What are you getting at?"

"Only one person, Roy Dunlap, could have put Quick up to the Sunset Farms visit. Maybe we flushed that covey of quail we were talking about."

Clayton's hand had unclenched and he smiled again. "I knew I picked the right man when I hired you. Then again, maybe you are way off base. Maybe those women over at the commune are doing the stealing."

"I can't agree with your paranoia, but if they are, I will find out about it."

Clayton pointed his finger at Buck. "Just git 'er done!" They were both laughing and walking out the door as Maria arrived with Buck's coffee. "We're finished in here. Bring it out to the veranda."

Buck followed Clayton as he hurried down the hallway. "You treat her like shit. Haven't you ever heard of please and thank you?"

"Women like to be told what to do. It's their lot in life."

Buck glanced up at the ceiling. "I hope your roof is

lightning-proof."

Clayton watched as Buck walked down the short flight of stairs to the Navigator.

"I'm on my way to the commune now."

"Good," Clayton said. "I sicked the Sheriff on them just for general principles. He should already be there."

***

It bothered Buck that Clayton had called the Sheriff and pointed a guilty finger at the women of Lykaia. He seriously doubted they were involved in any way. He also wondered why Lana wanted him to spend the night. His curiosity overflowing, he'd brought a change of clothes and had asked Hector to feed the horses and Pard while he was gone.

The roads were clear since the last time he'd visited. Unpaved roads in Logan County can become very slippery following rain or snow as he had experienced on more than one occasion. Today, because of sunshine and a steady breeze, he had no trouble tooling down the steep and narrow dirt road leading to the compound.

New oil well lease signs marked both sides of the road, attesting to drilling activity instigated by rising oil prices. Suddenly flush financially, he thought about asking Clayton to let him take a small interest in a well. As he mulled the idea, the front bumper of a police cruiser appeared from around a corner. It was the Logan County sheriff.

Sheriff Hagen, probably in his mid-fifties, had employed him more than once when he needed an extra deputy, or someone to help the death investigator inspect a crime scene. Buck stopped on the side of the road and waited for him to pull along side. Seeing the Navigator, Hagen parked the dark blue Dodge Charger in front of it.

Two inches shorter than Buck, Hagen had short-cropped black hair and a moustache. A former Army officer, he didn't like wearing uniforms. The badge, prominently displayed on his belt, was the only indication he was the most powerful law officer in Logan County.

"What are you up to?" Buck asked when the Sheriff stepped out of the car.

"Chasing cattle thieves. Got any in back of that pussy wagon of yours?"

Sheriff Hagen had a dry wit and rarely cracked a smile, but Buck knew he was enjoying his little joke.

"If I did, I wouldn't stop on the side of the road to chit-chat with the sheriff, now would I, Sheriff?"

Hagen flashed him another grin. "Guess not, but I can't say it for some of the genetic defects living around here. We busted a meth house about a block from the station last week."

It was Buck's turn to grin. They both knew use of crystal meth always resulted in diminished mental capacity, often making meth users and dealers their own worst enemies.

"I was just over at Clayton's. He said you would be checking out the compound to see if the women there stole his cattle."

Hagen shook his head and grinned again. "Clayton's my biggest political contributor. Whenever he asks me to check something out, I do it, no matter how stupid the request."

Buck nodded. "They don't strike me as criminal types."

"You're right about that. I was meaning to stop by, anyway. Someone's been harassing them. Mostly petty stuff but it could get serious if we don't do something about it."

Buck's ears perked. "What sort of stuff?"

"Someone running around harassing the women."

"Any ideas?"

"The usual suspects. Take a look." Sheriff Hagen rolled out a topographic map on the hood of the Charger. "Skeleton Creek runs right through Clayton's and the compound's property. There's a group of inbreeds and dope freaks living up the road, on the other side of Crescent. Whenever something like this happens, you can almost bet they are involved."

"Trey mentioned the place. Can you pin the theft of Clayton's cows on them?"

"I'm working on it."

"Two women in uniform stopped me at the gate last time I visited the commune," Buck said.

"They have their own security people, and do a pretty capable job. Still, I don't want a rape occurring over there."

Buck continued looking at the topo map. The Sheriff had oriented it so it faced north.

"There's no fence line between Clayton's place and the compound," he said. "Whoever stole the cows probably ran them down into the creek. The bottom is wide and flat, and mostly hidden by blackjacks growing on both sides. Unless I miss my guess, they herded them to an oil lease, loaded them into a trailer and took off with them."

Buck traced the course of Skeleton Creek with his index finger. "They probably went west, the direction of the nearest paved road. They could have gone anywhere once they reached Highway 74."

"Possibly to another county, outside my jurisdiction. Professional thieves know how to work the system."

"A flawed system," Buck said. "What'll we do?"

"Ask your buddy, Trey. He has the authority, no matter what county, or state, is involved."

"Trey said Roy Dunlap's ranch is north of Crescent. Is it near the biker community?"

Sheriff Hagen nodded. "Practically adjacent to one another. Why do you ask?"

Buck continued staring at Sheriff Hagen's topo map. "Just trying to get my bearings."

"Keep it," Hagen said. "I've got a dozen more back

at the office."

Buck saluted as Sheriff Hagen shut the door of the Logan County police cruiser behind him. "Thanks Sheriff," he said.

Hagen pointed his finger at Buck. "You stay out of trouble. I'm friends with the sheriffs of Payne, Lincoln and Oklahoma Counties, but you're out of luck if you get in trouble somewhere else."

"I'll do my best," Buck said with a grin.

He watched as Sheriff Hagen drove away down the section line road. Placing the topo map on the hood of his own truck, he glanced at it again. Skeleton Creek lay just over the hill and he made a mental note to return, maybe with Lady, and follow the creek to see where it led.

Chapter 9

Although he didn't know why Lana wanted him to spend the night at Lykaia, he maintained his fantasies about her possible intentions. He was thinking about it when the Lykaia police met him at the gate. They exchanged a few meaningless words as they collected his bag, abandoned the Navigator and proceeded to the main compound in their electric vehicle.

The two female officers escorted him to the concourse of tunnels beneath the commune, soon reaching an area resembling a hotel lobby. They pointed him to an attractive young woman standing behind what appeared to be a check-in counter.

"She'll take care of you from here."

Buck introduced himself to the smiling woman behind the counter.

"Of course, Mr. McDivit. Your room is ready and here is your key. Make yourself at home and someone will summon you later."

She handed him a plastic card with a magnetic strip and pointed him down the hall. As he keyed the door and entered, he wondered just how big the hotel was, and how many guests they usually had—a question he intended to ask Lana at the appropriate time.

Unlike any other hotel he had stayed in, this one had dim green lighting which flooded the interior with an ethereal glow. He sprawled on the bed, falling asleep and not waking until a knock on the door interrupted his vivid dream. Rubbing his eyes, he opened the door and stared at a friendly young woman, her hand extended in a business-like fashion.

"I'm Kristy. I'll be your guide tonight."

She was young, probably in her early twenties. Dark expressive eyes matched her raven hair and olive complexion, and highlighted teeth good enough for a toothpaste commercial. She followed him into the room, waiting while he stepped into the bathroom and returned with combed hair and a fresh shirt.

"What now?" he asked.

"Come with me," she said, providing him no explanation as he followed her down a long, concourse hallway.

They soon reached a restaurant he recognized as the same one he and Lana had dined the first night he had visited Lykaia. This time, Kristy left him alone at a table with a chilled bottle of Skeleton Creek Cabernet. Wondering about all the intrigue, he dined to the dulcet chords of the same string quartet as before, feeling euphoric after his first glass of wine. A half-hour passed before Kristy returned, seating herself in a chair across the candle-lit table from him.

"You're going to take part in a ceremony tonight."

"Lana didn't mention anything about a ceremony. I thought I was here to do some investigative work for her."

"I don't question Lana's intentions and I'm sure she has her reasons."

Underground for several hours, Buck had lost track of time and wondered if it was also part of Lana's intentions. Strangely affected by the wine, it didn't seem to matter to him.

He followed Kristy back down the underground

hallway to an opening leading to the surface. When they exited the tunnel system, he realized just how much the underground experience and wine had confused his psyche. The sky was dark, the day growing late.

Kristy led him through moonlit darkness for some distance, finally reaching an Indian teepee. She held the flap for him, waiting as he entered. A small fire burned in the center of the teepee, smoke rising upward and disappearing through an opening high above them. Feeling more than a bit detached from reality, he sensed he had imbibed something stronger than just wine. Whatever it was had elevated his euphoria and prevented him from caring.

"Take off your clothes and put on this breechcloth."

She handed him a deerskin breechcloth and a buckskin belt. She waited, not bothering to leave the tent or even turn her head while he undressed. In his state of elation, he didn't mind, even enjoying her voyeurism.

"We're not done. I need to paint you."

Buck sat on the stool, half-naked as Kristy painted his face and chest with ancient symbols whose meaning perhaps only she knew. When she finished, he looked like an Indian warrior, replete with war paint and head feathers. Pleased with her handiwork, Kristy flashed him a smile and then kissed him.

"What now?"

"Showtime," she said, grabbing his hand and leading him to the door of the teepee.

Snow and inclement weather of the previous week had vanished but goose bumps still popped up on his skin as they followed the moonlit trail toward percussive drumming of Indian tom-toms. They soon reached a clearing in the forest, a large bonfire burning and a hundred or more people, all women, sitting or standing around the fire.

Morning Mist of Blood

Only feathers and animal pelts clothed the mass of chanting females. Like Buck, colorful paints decorated their faces and exposed skin. Kristy escorted him to a small group of women, their extra feathers and adornments marking them as leaders. He also noticed someone he recognized. It was Georgia. She blew him a kiss as Kristy redirected his attention with a shove of the shoulder.

The most ornate female, he noted, was Lana, looking nothing like the corporate executive of their last meeting. She didn't speak when he stood before her, simply nodding for him to sit on the colorful serape draped on the ground beside her.

Waves of frenzied dancers moved into the circle, he observed with only the giddiest of perception. When offered, he drank from a cup passed around the circle, almost instantly feeling intoxicated. The drink numbed him and he, like the women around him, began swaying to the tom-tom's hypnotic rhythm. Drumming continued as half-naked women danced in and out of the circle. When Lana handed him a ceremonial pipe, he took a puff without thinking, psychedelic smoke rushing straight to his brain.

As the beat grew louder, dancing became ever more frenetic and sensual. Even in his drugged state, he realized he was participating in an ancient revel which had some intense meaning to the women dancing in and out of the circle lighted only by the center bonfire and the moon and stars. A stunning woman soon joined the other dancers. Tall, with long black hair extending to the crack of her well-turned derriere, she wore only a breechcloth, paint and feathers. The strange and intricate tattoo on her left shoulder blade, a pair of intertwined rattlesnakes with strange heads, only added to her exotic beauty.

Even in his extreme state of drug-induced euphoria, his mind did a double take. The woman carried a large rattlesnake, this one alive. Despite his mental condition, his eyes riveted on her erect nipples and the snake. She danced to a spot directly in front of him, thrusting the writhing reptile high into the air. Slowly, she lowered it, until its head resided directly in front of him. Zoned almost totally out, he stared into the viper's eyes as it jutted its pointed tongue a few inches from his face.

Whatever drug had invaded his brain had also removed any fear or anxiety about the reptile's danger. Like star-crossed lovers, they exchanged a kiss which would have curdled his blood, were he cognizant. He wasn't. The gorgeous woman released the serpent and it slithered away, into the darkness.

Prompted by some primeval urge, he stood from the serape and waded into the circle crowded again with chanting dancers, arms stretched to the sky, reveling in the proximity to so many half-naked females, his senses flooded by sound and the musky odor of burning wood and sweating bodies.

Women danced shoulder to shoulder, Buck among them. In his impaired state of mind, he watched Lana, half-naked and enjoying herself immensely, dancing sensually with Kristy. He forgot the images of Lana and Kristy, focusing on the drumming beat of Indian tom-toms and dozens of wildly chanting women. The revel continued throughout the night.

***

As a brilliant Oklahoma dawn greeted the eastern sky, the drumming and dancing ceased and all the women prostrated themselves on the ground. Soon, they were rolling in the dirt, laughing and carrying on as dust, kicked up by hours of frenzied dancing, covered their perspiring bodies. The frenzy ended when one of the dirt-coated women tore off her skimpy outfit and ran naked into the woods. Even coated with dust and dirt, Buck could see it was Lana. The other women ripped off their clothing and followed her. Caught up in the moment, he did the same. Lana led them to a large pond and completed a running dive off the wooden dock.

Buck and the women jumped in after her, the pond soon filled with naked females, laughing and squealing, water still icy after the recent snow. Cold water filled his spirit with feelings of revival and well-being. After washing sand and dirt off his skin and out of his hair and eyes, he followed the women as they began exiting the pond en masse.

They moved down the trail, back toward Lykaia, this time at a much easier pace. None of them seemed to notice Buck, or care he was as naked as they were. They departed the woods, reaching a recreational park where people met them with warm terrycloth robes. Temperatures were in the fifties but Buck's robe felt snug and comfortable after his chilly dip in the pond.

A feast had been set out on the picnic tables and he realized just how famished he was following the nightlong revel. Kristy found him in the crowd, grabbed his arm and led him to an empty seat next to Lana. She had a mouth filled with melon and motioned him to help himself to the virtual cornucopia of food on the table in front of them. He didn't need prompting.

The feast consisted of fruit, vegetables, juices and meat—everything probably grown on the compound or bartered from neighboring farms. Everyone was apparently as hungry as he was, doing lots of eating and little talking. Lana finally put down her knife and smiled at Buck.

"You survived the revel," she said.

"Yes, at least I think so. Do you do this often?"

When she shook her head, her crimson hair rippled in the sun. "It's the spring equinox. We celebrate the beginning of spring and give thanks for the bounty of the earth."

She grinned when he said, "I couldn't help but notice I am the only male present."

"You were an integral part of the revel. Even

though we are an all-female compound, we understand males occupy an important part of the universe. Last night you performed the role of Fertility Deity in our ritual. Thanks to you, the women of Lykaia will be healthy and fertile this year."

Buck's mouth opened slightly. "I thought you asked me here to assist you in an investigation."

Lana touched his hand." Of course, but I felt you might enjoy witnessing our celebration. You aren't offended, are you?"

"No, but you didn't have to drug me."

Still holding his hand, Lana squeezed. "There is no duplicity here. We all felt the same potency of the ceremonial drugs we use in our religion."

"I thought you were pagans."

"What I said was some people think of us as pagans. All religions have their roots in paganism. Easter has no set date but is determined by the cycles of the moon. The name Easter came from Eostre the Goddess of Fertility. Each year the children hunt eggs, a universal female symbol. Christmas began as a mid-winter celebration. Scandinavian pagans called the holiday Yule, a word now synonymous with Christmas. Shall I continue?"

Buck smiled and waved his hand. "I didn't intend anything negative by my comment."

"We actually consider our religion more closely aligned with early Native Americans."

"Like the Southern Death Cult?"

"You have done your homework. Our religion celebrates the earth. We are no more than occupants of the universe and do our best never to take more than we return in kind. It's a simple concept, but one we believe is all important.

"Religion aside, maybe it's time to tell me what you are hiring me for."

"As I said, Lykaia has a problem."

"Please tell me about it."

Lana closed her eyes and put her hands to her temples. "A strange person is harassing Lykaia."

"What has he done?" Buck prompted.

"Nothing serious, at least not yet."

"You have an ID on this person?"

"A large and very powerful man. He seems to be watching us, as he has accosted two women as they did things on the surface."

"Like what?"

"He frightened them when he appeared from out of the woods. He grabbed one of our commune members and tried to force himself on her. He didn't rip her clothes or anything, but his actions were sexually overt and frightened her."

"Has he compromised your underground buildings?"

"He may have tried, but he hasn't succeeded."

"I suppose none of your people carry weapons."

Lana drew a breath and shook her head. "Although we are non-violent people, our police carry weapons. Do you carry a gun, Mr. McDivit?"

Buck shook his head. "I did when I was a cop, but not anymore."

"Then maybe you don't believe in violence either."

"I'm a big man. Potential attackers know they could get hurt if they pick a fight."

Lana frowned. "The women of Lykaia don't have that luxury. We could be victims and I can not allow it."

"But you have an effective police force. Don't they provide a deterrent to your stalker?"

"They've searched for the man but he is cunning and seems to know his way around the forest. I am sure if we don't act, it's just a matter of time before he does something horrible. Can you help us?"

"I'll do what I can. Where do you suggest I start?"

"Esme is our spiritual advisor. I'd like for you to talk with her first."

Lana grinned when Buck said, "I'm at your

service."

When a pretty young woman joined them, it became apparent to Buck the two women were a couple. His fantasies of a possible romantic relationship with the redheaded beauty flew out the window. Following a more-than friendly hug and kiss, she introduced the woman to him.

"This is Sara. We have an appointment. Kristy will take you to see Esme."

After the feast, Kristy led Buck to his hotel room. "We had a tiring night. Take a nap and I will return later."

***

When Kristy and Buck exited the underground complex much later, he was surprised it was after dark. Solar lamps lighted the narrow pathway they followed into the woods. Lights soon disappeared but Kristy apparently knew the way. It wasn't far to the small clearing occupied by the same large buckskin teepee he had used as a dressing room the previous night. Kristy opened the flap, entering without verbally acknowledging their arrival. Lit by a small fire and a few candles, the inside of the teepee shined with an ephemeral glow, a woman Buck instantly recognized waiting in the dimness for them.

"I'm Buck McDivit."

She didn't bother shaking his hand or explain why. After a pregnant pause, he just stood there, waiting for her response, good or bad.

"You're a handsome man, even with all your clothes on," she finally said.

"Thanks," Buck said. "At least I guess."

"I am Esme, high-priestess of Lykaia."

Esme was the beautiful woman with the rattlesnake tattoo who danced nearly naked during the ceremony. As he stood close enough to touch her, he felt his skin grow warm. The sensation passed up from his loins, to his neck. His face felt as if it had turned red.

When she smiled, he was sure of it.

A sound behind him, the low growl of an animal which was not quite a dog, caused the hair to stand up on the back of his neck. Turning his head, he saw the bared fangs of a large beast that looked like a wolf.

"I would advise you not to make any abrupt moves. Beauty isn't a full-blood wolf but she's close enough. The dog in her only seems to exacerbate her temperament."

Moving slowly, he faced the creature and knelt down so they were at face level. Then he rolled on his back and spread his arms. Beauty whimpered and took a cautious step toward him, finally licking his face. Raising his head, Buck kissed the wolf dog on its fanged muzzle.

"You got a set of balls on you," Esme said. "But I guess I already had that part figured out."

Buck grasped the large beast's neck and hugged it. The wolf dog wasn't wagging its tail but it was obvious she was already enamored by the big cowboy. Standing behind them and suddenly unable to resist the two wrestling on the floor, Kristy joined them.

"This gorgeous animal's name is Beauty?" Buck asked.

"You apparently have a sixth sense of which I wasn't aware," Esme said.

"She is a beauty," Buck said.

"If you three can pull away from your frivolity, I think we have a matter to discuss."

Buck quit scratching behind Beauty's ears and glanced up at Esme.

"I'm at your service," he said.

Esme grinned. "That's what I like hearing a man say. Let's take a dip in the hot tub and relax. We can talk there."

Buck and Kristy followed Esme out the flap of the teepee to a large wooden tub, barely illuminated by moon and starlight. Stripping naked, she climbed the stairs up to the deck surrounding the tub, dipped a cautious toe into hot water, and then immersed herself up to her neck. Kristy needed no prompting. Doffing her clothes, she joined Esme in the wooden hot tub, bringing with her a large jug of wine and a covered basket. Buck hesitated in taking off his clothes.

"Don't be bashful," Esme said. "You weren't last night and we have both already seen you naked."

Although fraught with feelings of impropriety, he removed his clothes and eased into the hot water, fingers of steam wisping up from its surface.

"Where is the heat coming from?"

"The tub is wood-fired. I have no electricity here."

"It's wonderful. I've never sat in a hot tub beneath the stars before."

"There is nothing else like it in the world."

His passions ignited by hot water and naked bodies, Buck closed his eyes, luxuriating in the attention the two gorgeous women were giving him.

Feeling a little left out, Beauty issued a plaintiff howl at the hazy moon.

Buck finally relaxed, feeling more comfortable when water had covered most of his body.

"Maybe you should tell me about the stalker before I fall asleep."

"If you do, Esme and I will have our egos shattered," Kristy said.

Buck grinned. "I was exaggerating. I'm relaxed but there is no way I could fall asleep."

Kristy removed the cork from the jug of wine, tipped it over her shoulder and drank a healthy slug. Esme followed her lead and then handed the bottle to Buck.

"This isn't going to make me do strange things, is it?"

"It depends on how you are affected by cheap red wine," Esme said.

Buck tipped the bottle over his shoulder and drank

as distant lightning flashed across the sky.

Kristy and Esme laughed when he said, "This doesn't taste like Skeleton Creek Cabernet."

"Potent wine isn't always expensive. A spring storm is coming," Esme said. "Do you believe in spirits?"

"I saw a ghost once."

"Are you sure it was a ghost?"

"I was drunk, but I believe what I saw was the ghost of a girl who had died because of unexplained reasons."

"I'm glad you have an open mind. Most would deny their own eyes."

"Why are you asking me about ghosts?"

"Not ghosts, a spirit. Lana's stalker is a being from a different plane of reality. It wanders the creeks and hills, searching for something."

"Like what?"

"I don't know. The spirit assumes the shape of a muscular black man."

"But he hasn't harmed anyone."

Esme shook her head. "No, but he has frightened at least two residents of Lykaia."

"You two are creeping me out," Kristy said, reaching into the covered basket and removing three brownies. "It's giving me a powerful hunger for something sweet."

Kristy took one of the large brownies and handed the other two to Buck and Esme.

"Pot-laced," Esme said when Buck bit into the chewy treat. "But don't worry. There isn't enough there to do any damage."

Approaching storms continued moving toward them. The sky, at least for the moment was luminous, with glowing stars and a golden moon which was almost full. A familiar voice interrupted Esme's tale of the errant spirit.

"We want our share," someone said from the

darkness.

It was Sara and Lana.

"We came for a soak and we have good wine, not Esme's cheap swill."

Wine and pot were already working on him when Lana and Sara shed their clothes and joined them in the hot tub. Lana, the buttoned-down business person, had the looks of a movie star and body of a stripper. He had almost gotten used to being nude with the gorgeous women when she touched his thigh.

Kristy doused the torches, the lack of ambient light affording them a perfect view of moon and stars, along with flickering fireflies lighting the clearing. Up to their chests in hot water, he felt less naked and more at ease. This all changed when Kristy sat in his lap and put her arm around his shoulder. Sara, Esme and Lana smiled, enjoying Buck's discomfort.

"Relax," Sara said. "We won't bite you."

"Speak for yourself," Kristy said, nibbling his ear.

Buck tried not to become sexually aroused, failing miserably. No one seemed to mind, or even notice. The bold red native wine and pot-laced brownies had anesthetized him and released him of all inhibitions.

An Oklahoma spring storm approached, distant thunder sounding ever closer. A south breeze scattered fingers of steam rising off hot water. Wind intensified, along with rain dappling the hot tub's surface. He remembered following the women out of the water, and little else.

Chapter 10

Buck's psyche descended into a dream world, some place other than here and now. Darkness cloaked him like a damp blanket. Still quite naked, he trod barefoot along a narrow trail surrounded by trees which blocked moon and starlight. Something lay ahead, waiting for him. He stopped, not wanting to proceed, but knew he had to.

His dream transmuted into a different time and place. Still dark, he lay on a thick bearskin rug, naked Esme kneeling behind him, stroking his shoulders and neck with deft fingers. The flap of the teepee opened and three women entered—Sara and Kristy on either side of Lana. All three women were naked except for the stole of colorful feathers cloaking Lana.

Flickering firelight illuminated the teepee, allowing Buck to perceive reality, or his perception of it in blurry shadows. Incense filled his nostrils with the odor of cloves, mingling with Lana's perfume and her woman-smell as she approached him. She followed his eyes, long legs spread wide as Kristy and Sara removed the cloak of feathers, red hair on her head and pubic region almost green in the eerie light of Esme's glimmering fire. Slowly bending her long dancer's legs, she straddled him.

His dream began moving seamlessly between very different events. Esme's fire disappeared, replaced by darkness of a forest path. Sharp pebbles gouged his feet as he inched toward shadows beyond a bend. An unknown being, large and frightening, waited for him, yet something continued to draw him toward the darkness.

Lana lay beneath him again, her pale blue eyes rolling, along with her body moving to the crescendo of a mental orchestra. Esme, Kristy and Sara kneeled around them, chanting and laying on hands as Buck and Lana made passionate love in the teepee's muted light.

"Who are you?" Buck asked as he stared at the dark man in his path.

The strange and powerful being he might be, didn't answer.

"Let me pass," Buck said, stepping forward until stopped by strong hands.

"Where is the man with the two blonde women?" the dark man demanded.

"Buck shook his head. "Let me pass."

With eyes glowing supernatural green, the wraith squeezed Buck's shoulders until they ached.

"Tell me."

"I don't know what you're talking about."

"Yes you do. You must lead me to the dog killer."

***

Buck awoke wrapped in a colorful Indian rug on the floor of Esme's teepee. Beauty had a mouthful of the rug, yanking on it to get his attention. Patting her head, he rubbed behind her ears, dim memories of making passionate love to Kristy and Esme seeming almost like a dream, but not quite.

"Morning, big girl. Where's your Mama?"

As if to show him, Beauty walked to the door, gazed out and then returned. Buck grinned when he pulled away the blanket and realized he was quite naked. He had little memory of what had happened after leaving the hot tub, except for the muted recollection of Kristy and Esme's warm bodies. Something else had happened but he couldn't remember what it was. It didn't seem to matter because he felt wonderfully alive and stoked beyond imagination.

"This may be the best job I've ever had," he said as he hunted for his clothes.

Esme entered the tent as he was dressing. "Leaving so early? You told me last night you would stay with me forever."

"Yeah, well if I don't get up and do something, Miss Lana will run me off. Then I'd never see you again."

"Kristy was worried about the same thing and left before the sun came up."

Mention of Kristy assured Buck he wasn't dreaming and had indeed spent the night with two gorgeous women.

"You're okay about last night?" he asked. "I mean about the three of us, and all?"

"No problem, and I'm sure Kristy doesn't mind either. It isn't as if you never made love to us before. You performed ritual love with most of the women of Lykaia at the ceremony."

"Maybe in my dreams. Unless . . . . What exactly did I do at the ritual the other night?"

"You were the only man present. What do you think you did?"

Buck rubbed his palm across the rough stubble of his morning beard. "Please tell me I didn't have sex with a hundred different women."

Esme grinned again. "Of course not, but lets say your manhood was on prominent display. Don't worry, there were no videos made."

It was Buck's turn to grin. "Too bad because I would pay good money to see it."

Kristy stuck her head in the flap. Having overheard the last snippet of conversation, she said, "Is someone talking about me?"

"No, but you were next on our list."

"Are you ready to start the investigation?"

"I'm wearing the same clothes I came here in. Any chance for a shower?"

"Maybe, if you let me watch," she said.

"Why not? You already know me better than almost anyone."

***

Kristy didn't watch as Buck showered and changed clothes, waiting instead for him at the Tiers. Once alone, he called Hector Ramirez on his cell phone and apologized for the length of the assignment. He found Kristy sipping orange juice at a cozy table. They had breakfast and discussed where to begin.

"Constable Pruitt is chief of security in Lykaia. She has the straight skinny up to now."

"Is she going to corroborate Esme's spirit story?"

"Maybe you should ask her yourself."

Buck followed her down the underground passageway, glad she knew where she was going. When they reached a stairway leading to the surface, she sprinted up the steps.

"Now I know why everyone around here is in such good shape."

"Walking is wonderful exercise but we also have scenic trails for jogging and biking, and several tennis courts. Some of the women here are very good players. We also have a large indoor exercise facility."

"What about doctors?"

"We have a fully-staffed clinic with many of the amenities of a small hospital."

The police station was a partially aboveground building with a garage area for their strange vehicles. Banks of solar panels sat on the roof, apparently generating electricity to power them. He also noticed a windmill, its giant rotor turning slowly in an Oklahoma breeze.

"Is there anything you don't have here?"

Kristy grinned and said, "Men."

As they entered the building's front door, Buck wondered if it housed any jail cells. Shaped like a circle, a half-dozen offices ringed the central area where a woman resided behind a desk on a raised platform. An officer sat at a central control panel, observing images on several LED screens. Around the platform were bulletin boards with various notices similar to most police stations. He was staring at one when someone spoke his name.

"You must be Mr. McDivit."

He turned, expecting to see a large woman, perhaps slightly overweight, with short hair. The petite person did have short brown hair, and the nose and eyes of an enchanted pixie. Nothing else matched his expectations.

"I'm Ava Pruitt," she said, shaking his hand. "Please follow me."

The door to Constable Pruitt's office was open, with no intimidating secretary sitting in front. A desk, coffee pot, maps and aerial photos on the walls, populated the neat office.

"Have a seat," she said, motioning to the two chairs in front of her desk. "I've been waiting for you." The constable had files she opened and began going over with Buck and Kristy. "The male interloper made contact with two individuals. They were debriefed about their encounters and all had one thing in common."

"Please tell me."

"They gave different descriptions of the man, but agreed on the fact he was big and very muscular."

"We both know how unreliable eyewitness descriptions are. Any physical evidence?"

"Lykaia is encircled with buried wire that sounds

an alarm here at the station whenever someone crosses it. We don't know how he has entered without setting off the alarm. We took statements, if you'd like to read them."

They waited as Buck scanned the two documents. "I'd like to interview these women. Is it possible?" Sensing Pruitt's reticence, he asked, "Is something wrong?"

"We have state-of-the art surveillance cameras. Our officers are well trained and equipped. I am a graduate of the Oklahoma City Police Academy and have years of experience. It is beyond me why you think you can add to our already thorough investigation."

"I don't mean to step on any toes," he said. "I see by your reports you have done a thorough investigation. If I'd realized as much before I took the job, I would have told Lana she already has the best people working on the problem."

Ava winced when she heard Lana's name. Realizing she may have crossed a precarious line, she backtracked.

"The women are waiting outside. Do you require a separate room?"

"They'll both be more comfortable if you are here. Can we see them one at a time?"

An officer ushered in the first woman. Like Kristy, she was young, her slender body indicating her love of exercise. Ava pointed to the empty chair between her and Buck.

"This is Mr. McDivit. He is an outside investigator consulting with us and has some questions about your encounter with the man."

Buck nodded. "Please tell me what happened."

The mousy-haired woman named Jan had darting eyes which seemed unwilling to focus on Buck. As she repeated the first account he had read, she kept glancing around the room, and at Ava and Kristy.

"It was almost dark and everything happened so fast I didn't get a good look at him, not to mention he scared the daylights out of me."

"You said he was running when you first saw him. Was he on a casual jog, maybe enjoying the trail?"

Jan shook her head. "He wasn't jogging, he was sprinting, an ugly frown on his face and wild look in his eyes. What frightened me most was his total nudity."

Buck glanced at Ava at this titillating bit of information she had failed to share with him.

"Was he chasing something or maybe running away?"

"I have no idea."

There was a large map of the area on one of the walls. "Show me where you saw him."

Joining Buck in front of the map, she pointed emphatically to the location of the encounter.

"Here."

"It was dark. How can you be so sure?"

"The path has distance markers along the route. I had just punched the memory button on my runner's watch at the 10-K position. It's marked right here," Jan said, pointing again.

Buck scratched his chin as he pondered the map. "Describe him again for me."

"A large, heavily muscled black man."

Buck dismissed Jan, having gleaned about as much information from her as he could have hoped. He didn't comment as they awaited the second witness, a petite woman with a thick mane of springy curls that gave him the instant impression she was very young. Closer inspection signaled he was probably wrong by at least ten years.

"My name is Lily," she said.

"Please tell us about the man on the trail?" Ava prompted.

"Again?"

"It's my fault," Buck said. "I apologize for the

stress we're causing you but I think I can help and I need to hear your story myself."

Taken by the handsome cowboy, Lily's defensive demeanor changed almost instantly.

"I was jogging on the perimeter trail when a man appeared in the path before me. I was in a runner's high and paying little attention, except for the exhilaration I felt. I ran right into him and he wrapped his big arms around me."

"Did he try to accost you?"

"No, he grabbed my shoulders and shook me, demanding I take him to the blonde sisters, and the dog killer."

The woman's words rang a bell in Buck's subconscious mind. "What do you make of it?"

Ava shook her head. "We haven't a clue."

"I told him I didn't know what he was talking about."

"What did he do then?" Buck asked, returning his attention to Lily.

"Nothing really, but he had wild eyes which frightened me."

"Did you think he was going to harm you?"

Tears appeared in the corners of Lily's eyes. "He scared the shit out of me but I never thought he had any malicious intentions."

"Where did he go?"

"I was too frightened to look. I was afraid he would return so I crawled into the trees and hid until I was sure he was gone, and then ran back to Lykaia."

"Can you show us on this map where the attack took place?"

She pointed to a spot near the one Jan had indicated. When she was gone, Buck glanced at Ava and Kristy

"What about your surveillance cameras? Did they catch any of the action?"

Ava nodded. "Would you like to see them?"

They walked outside to the kiosk with the many LED screens.

"Please play back the two encounters with the interloper."

Without replying, the woman at the desk began typing information on the keyboard. The picture on the screen disappeared, replaced by the woman named Jan jogging down the lighted trail. The video showed her stopping abruptly, obviously disturbed by something in front of her. Her body jerked, her wild expression indicating something was causing her intense anxiety. Her gyrations were obvious, but the only other image captured was a flickering, ephemeral light.

"That is the strangest thing I have ever seen," Buck said. "It's almost like she sees . . . ."

"A ghost?"

Buck nodded and asked to see the second video. What they saw was much the same as the first—a frightened woman reacting to an ephemeral light which danced across the screen and finally disappeared.

"Now what do you think?" Ava asked.

Something the two women had told Buck sounded strangely familiar but he couldn't put his finger on what it was. Sightings of the man at the compound occurred only a few days before the murder at Clayton's ranch, and the cattle theft. A voice in his brain told him there was likely a connection.

Buck shook his head. "I'm not sure if we should call in a psychiatrist, or the Ghost Busters."

Ava didn't laugh.

Chapter 11

Buck thanked Hector for covering his feeding duties and watching Pard. The young Mexican with a noticeable limp, and prominent Spanish accent simply shrugged and smiled.

"Hey, no problem. You help me out plenty, and me and LaDona love Pard."

"He is a good dog. I got you something for your trouble." Buck gave him a bottle of Jack Daniel's. He grinned when Buck added, "I know you like tequila better, but I got you Black Jack instead."

Hector, Buck knew, didn't like tequila and it was a mark of their friendship they could joke about ethnic stereotypes. Lady whinnied and shook her head to show her pleasure when he finally reached her stall.

"How's my Lady?" he asked, petting her regal neck before giving her a mighty hug.

Lady was more happy to see him than annoyed by his disregard. She was also eager for a run. Buck didn't disappoint, saddling and leading her out of the barn. They spent the better part of the morning galloping along a riding trail, Pard matching them stride for stride.

Pard raced between his feet as he washed and groomed Lady before returning the beautiful horse to her stall. It was only then he thought about what he needed to do in order to proceed with the investigation. Pulling out the topo map Sheriff Hagen had given him, he located Clayton's ranch with his finger. Skeleton Creek lay just north of the house and he traced the course he and Clayton had taken in the Jeep to view the dead cow.

An oil well pumped Oklahoma crude slowly from the ground at a nearby oil lease. The lease, like the dead cow, lay just north of Skeleton Creek and connected to a section line road. A notation on the road indicated the little town of Crescent was ten miles further north.

Not far, at least as the crow flies, from the spot where Clayton had found the dead cow, was Lykaia, entered from a lease road which ran east off the very same section line road that continued on to Crescent. Buck wanted to check things on the ground and considered loading Lady into his horse trailer and taking her with him to Clayton's.

"You better stay and watch out for Hector, LaDona and the baby," he said, rubbing Pard's ears.

Buck also left Lady at Sunset Farms, knowing Clayton had plenty of horses. By now, his hands knew Buck was working for him and didn't detain him at the front gate. It was already late afternoon and he found Clayton strolling alone along a path in his Japanese garden.

"What's up?" he asked.

"I want to check out a few things on the north end of your ranch. Do you have a map and a horse I can borrow?"

"You know I have a hundred horses but I got something even better."Clayton took his cell phone from his shirt pocket. "Garth, bring me a ranch map. I'm headed for the motor pool."

Buck followed him down the winding path, suddenly aware many of the plants had started to bloom, Clayton's garden ablaze with the colors and odors of early spring. They exited the garden through a rustic gate. Another path led to a large metal building. Clayton pointed a device at the overhead door, an electric engine slowly raising it to reveal a dozen or more four-wheelers.

"I never got on one of these contraptions myself but the boys use them to check the fences and outlying pastures. They get more work done now and in less time. Take one."

Familiar with the vehicles, Buck had ridden one once with friends. They were all the same, even painted with Clayton's ranch colors of orange and black. He picked the one closest to the front door, straddled it and turned the key as Clayton's foreman joined them.

"This is Garth Dunlap."

Buck shook the man's hand, realizing he was the younger brother of Roy Dunlap. He could see the resemblance. Missing was Roy's buttoned-down image, replaced by the weathered skin of a man who had spent much of his life outdoors. A man with a distinctive baby face joined them, handing Garth a map.

"I made a copy like you said. Need anything else?"

"No, Johnny, that'll do it."

The man cast a quizzical glance at Buck before returning the way he came.

"Just follow this road. It'll take you to the north pastures," Garth said.

Handing Buck the map, he walked away behind the cowpoke named Johnny.

Buck watched him disappear around the corner and then asked, "Was that Johnny Crabtree?"

"Yep, not much of a hand if you ask me, but Garth likes him."

Cranking the four-wheeler, he headed up the path. Once out of sight, he stopped and examined the map Garth Dunlap had given him, apparently a copy Johnny Crabtree had made from the original. The handwritten words—Garth's map—occupied its upper left hand corner. He also noticed several markings and notations, one of them on the fence line of the very pasture where he had assisted in investigating the murdered man. A good place to start, he decided.

All the gates had numerous locks, linked so anyone who regularly used the gates had a key, or combination, to his own lock. Garth's map provided combinations for his locks and Buck had no trouble navigating the maze of gates and pathways to Clayton's northernmost fence.

The ATV had lots of muscle, enough to easily power a two-hundred pound man down the road at more than fifty miles per hour. Still early spring, a slight breeze and the nip in the air made him glad he had worn his sleeveless down parka. He followed the fence line until he reached the penciled x mark Clayton's foreman had made. Finding the general location, he began walking the fence, looking for some reason Garth had marked it. He soon found what he was looking for.

To the unsuspecting eye, the section of fence was no different from the rest of the barrier. Closer inspection revealed something else entirely. Someone had rigged it in such a way that it would swing open with little effort. Without knowledge of the secret gate's location, it looked normal. The marking on the map made Garth a prime suspect in the rustling of Clayton's cows. After another glance at his topo map, he stared at the tree line marking the course of Skeleton Creek.

Buck headed north through the hidden gate in Clayton's fence. When he reached the tree line, he turned westward, searching for a trail leading down to the creek. He soon found the spot he was looking for. Once through the narrow breach, he slid the ATV down the steep bank. The big tires of the sure-footed vehicle would have made a potentially treacherous descent to the creek easy. It didn't matter because someone had modified the steep bank, lessening the angle down to the water. Someone also likely involved in the cattle theft.

A spring storm was brewing in the west, a wall cloud darkening the sky. Buck hadn't checked the weather report before leaving Sunset Farms and had no idea how severe the storm might be. It didn't really matter because if you lived in Oklahoma long enough, you knew the weather was always subject to abrupt change.

Tracks of both horses and cattle marked the mud and dirt around the creek bed. He had no trouble tracking them as they turned in a westerly direction. Overhanging limbs of trees on both sides of the creek formed a roof-like enclosure, resulting in a darkened tunnel. The approaching storm made the path even darker, causing him to switch on the vehicle's lone headlamp.

Buck didn't bother stopping to check the topo map because he felt sure the path of the cattle headed toward the oil lease located just north of Skeleton Creek. Hundreds of creeks, some large and some small, dissect central Oklahoma. Many remain almost dry during much of the year, but carry lots of water during the spring and fall rainy seasons. Skeleton Creek was no different. Larger than most and always carrying some water, it often became a roaring torrent during periods of heavy rainfall.

Buck soon found the spot where the rustlers had driven the cattle out of the creek bed. Again, he had no trouble powering the ATV up the slope. The first thing he saw upon exiting the tree line was a lone oil well pumping unit, its polished rod screeching as it moved slowly up and down.

The sky had darkened noticeably, a fine mist of rain beginning to fall. A lease fence encircled the pumping unit. Oil leases are dangerous places and pump jacks heavy pieces of constantly moving machinery. Because of this, Oklahoma law requires oil operators to maintain a security fence around them and to keep them locked.

Buck soon solved the puzzle. Prompted by his discovery at Clayton's ranch, he scanned the back of the fence for just such an entry, his search soon rewarded. Pulling back a hidden gate, he entered the lease with ease.

Most oil leases are usually bare dirt paved with just enough gravel to allow access to large trucks. The sky was growing darker by the minute but Buck could easily see hoof prints of horses, and the cattle someone had herded there from Clayton's ranch. Whoever had used the oil lease to load the stolen cattle was also someone who had access to the well. The sign fronting the oil tanks pegged Crescent Oil Company as the owner. Buck wasn't surprised.

The map unwittingly provided by Garth Dunlap, implicated him in the rustling. His brother Roy, the president of Crescent Oil, had access to the lease and could easily have supplied a key or combination to get the cattle trailer in and out of the front gate. Buck had little time to ponder Garth and Roy's complicity in the theft as rain continued falling, lightly at first and then in a pelting torrent. Resetting the fence, he straddled the ATV and started back toward Clayton's ranch.

Oklahoma red clay provides firm footing during dry weather, but becomes treacherously slick when rain begins. Buck realized as much as he tracked his path back to Skeleton Creek. The formerly gentle flow had reverted to a swirling torrent of rushing water, probably exacerbated by flooding upstream.

ATVs are sure-footed vehicles. Still, when he pointed its wheels down the slope, he realized he had made a mistake. The front end slipped sideways, out of control, and then flipped over, dumping him into slick mud. The work someone had done to lessen the slope to the creek had also compromised its integrity. Water poured down the opening, washing away any traction which may have existed. For Buck, it didn't matter as he tumbled toward moving water, the ATV rolling on top of him.

The weight of the little vehicle carried him into the torrent Skeleton Creek had suddenly become, and rushing water propelled him rapidly downstream. He had swallowed lots of water and his muscles felt like warm putty when he finally grabbed a log lodged against the bank and pulled himself up the slippery slope, somewhat out of the water.

Rain continued to fall but the brunt of the rapidly moving storm had already passed over. He lay in the mud for a while, spitting up water and trying to catch his breath. When his strength finally returned, he found he had another problem.

Mud was so slick it sucked one of his boots right off of his foot. When he tried to stand, his feet came out from under him and he plunged back into the muck. Finally reaching the relative stability of a red sandstone boulder, he stretched out on his back and drew an exhausted breath.

As he rested on the rock, the storm abated, replaced by darkness. It made the creek bed seem almost like the inside of a cave. Using roots and stone, he finally managed to work himself above the rushing water. What he found was a game trail, established by decades, maybe even centuries, of wild animals.

Supported by rock and roots, the narrow pathway provided his first sure footing since exiting the oil lease. He was drenched, his cap gone, along with one of his favorite boots, and he had to pick his way on the trail because it was too dark to see. He also had the uneasy feeling something was tracking him.

Chapter 12

Buck continued along the narrow game trail, apprehensive he might lose his footing and tumble back into the raging water. He had no other option as very little light filtered through the roof of interlocking branches. Something in the distance, an animal coughing to let creatures in the forest know it was on the prowl, also raised his anxiety level. The eerie sound caused a sudden increase in his heart rate. Even though he had never heard it before, he knew it was Clayton's panther.

Whumph. The throaty cough echoed down the narrow valley formed by Skeleton Creek. The beast was close, but because of darkness and resonance of sound, he couldn't tell just how close. Groping for a branch or rock to use as a weapon, he found nothing.

Subdued rain continued to fall but the sound of gusting wind was at times almost deafening, instantly lowering the pressure in the arboreal tunnel whenever a blow began. Lacking vision, his hearing and sense of smell compensated. He could almost taste the loamy odor of thick mud coating his body. He also sensed another storm was approaching.

Having lost track of time, he knew Clayton would soon miss him, and send out a search party. With this in mind, he yelled "Hello." Nothing but the roar of gusting wind answered him.

Muscles aching from exhaustion, he wanted only to hunker down and wait until morning. The cough of the panther caused him to decide differently. He continued picking his way along the slope until a scream behind him chilled his soul. Turning, he faced the monster he couldn't see but was close enough for him to smell.

He had heard panthers make a noise like the scream of a woman. Now he knew it was true. He also realized the panther wanted him to make his presence known, and he could only imagine the beast in a crouch, fangs bared, ready to spring and tear him to shreds. Within seconds, his nightmare became all too real.

The weight of the heavy cat hammered him into the mud. Jaws would have clamped his jugular, holding him in place with two large paws until his last breath escaped from his body, but Buck had ducked and pivoted, the beast's claws raking only his back. Having no other weapon, he grabbed a double handful of mud, thrusting it into the panther's eyes.

Some primeval instinct guided his hands, the panther howling in outrage when struck in the face with the globs of sticky mud. The ruse worked for only a moment, but long enough for him to dive down the ledge to the creek.

The fall should have knocked him silly, except he landed in shallow water. Plowing ahead, his heart beat double-time as his mind raced for answers, knowing the panther would be on him in a flash. The water wasn't deep, but flowing rapidly and he let the current carry him forward. He couldn't hear the big cat but somehow knew it was bounding after him. When he reached solid ground, he sprang to his feet and began running toward light, maybe from the moon, in the roof of the arboreal tunnel. He didn't make it very far.

Tripping on a pile of brush, he slid to a painful halt

in fine sand and gravel. Turning, he saw the panther for the first time. Like a monster, its eyes glowed red in muted moonlight, muscles rippling in its powerful frame. The big cat was solid black.

Scooping a handful of gravel, he tossed it at the beast, his efforts doing nothing to slow the cat's movement toward him. Having no other weapon, he threw another handful of gravel and then waited for the cat to lunge, unable to move because of a twisted ankle. Hearing a mortal growl directly behind him, he turned to see Beauty, Esme's giant wolf dog. Stepping in front of him, she braced for the cat's attack. Beauty was big, but not nearly as big as the panther. Still, she crouched with lowered head and bared fangs, dancing from side to side, daring the cat to attack her. He soon did, missing her neck as he rolled her in the creek bottom.

Beauty didn't miss his, but failed to catch the jugular. She had the big cat by the back of its neck, painful but not lethal. The panther turned on its back, bucking and flailing its claws, trying to shake the powerful animal off its neck. Buck continued groping in the semi-darkness, finally finding a heavy piece of driftwood. Hoping not to strike Beauty, he dived on the two beasts, nailing the big cat between the eyes, and then continuing to swing.

The panther could have taken either Buck or Beauty alone, but not both. Managing to clip her head with one large paw, it backed away, snarling, and then disappeared into the darkness. Buck lay exhausted, his arms around the huge wolf dog. Beauty was on the ground, her muscles twitching and breath coming in labored gasps. His hands were sticky with the ooze of warm blood—his, Beauty's, the panther's, or maybe all three. Tearing off what remained of his shirt, he stuffed it into the gaping wound in the big wolf dog's side and applied pressure.

***

Buck had lost all concept of time when someone

shook his shoulder. He stared up into Esme's mystical eyes. Stuffing something into his mouth, she told him to swallow it.

"You are hurt, but not as badly as Beauty. I gave you something for the pain. Now you need to help me with her."

"How did you find us?"

Her smile flashed in muted moonlight. "Our thoughts are connected in a subconscious collective. You called for help, and I came."

Her explanation made him grin. Whatever drug she had given him had already begun working. Releasing his grip on the big wolf dog, he raised himself into a sitting position. Esme began working on Beauty. The big cat had raked bloody claw marks across her right side, and had left an opened wound on her head. After removing what was left of Buck's shirt from the wound, she dabbed it with a medicine-coated rag and then bound it tightly with a large bandage. Slipping a pill into Beauty's mouth, she massaged the animal's throat until she swallowed it.

"The pill is more than medicine and will give both of you a physical boost. I'll lead us out of here but you'll need to help her along."

When Beauty rose up on her haunches, Buck hugged her, though careful not to do further damage.

"You saved my life," he said, kissing her.

They spent the next hour slowly hiking to Esme's teepee. The storm had blown over, leaving only wispy clouds which now barely cloaked twinkling stars and hazy moon. Crickets and tree frogs had begun singing, and they could still hear the panther in the distance. When they reached her encampment, Esme took them inside and handed him a ladle of water.

"Wait while I cleanse Beauty's wounds. She's in much worse shape than you are."

Buck sipped water laced with medicine Esme thought would help him and waited as she worked on the big animal.

"Will she make it?" he asked when she finally returned to check on him.

"The cat hurt her badly and she has lost lots of blood. She would have died if you hadn't staunched the flow with your shirt."

"I'll feel horrible if she doesn't pull through."

Esme smiled. "She'll make it. She has a big heart. I stitched her wounds and gave her medicine and herbs to start the healing process."

"You're a wonder woman."

"Now it's your turn. Come outside and lets get the rest of your clothes off."

Buck had no clue how stiff his muscles had become until he tried to stand. A big woman, Esme pulled him to his feet. and then helped him outside to a makeshift shower. She stripped away what remained of his muddy clothes and he stood naked beneath a canvas water bag as she bathed him with a sponge.

"You need stitches in your shoulder," she said when she finished washing away the last of the caked blood and mud. "The cat really nailed you. I'm surprised you got away from it."

"No one more surprised than me. I was about ready to kiss my ass goodbye when Beauty showed up."

"I doubt it, Buck McDivit. You don't have an ounce of quit in your body."

Esme kissed him, gave him another painkiller and then sewed up the wound on his shoulder. After administering a healing balm, she bandaged it securely.

"Now," she said. "I have one last potion for you."

Esme gave him a goblet filled with a semi-sweet liquid he could not identify.

"What is it?"

"An aphrodisiac. No way I'm taking a gorgeous hunk of man to bed with me unless he can perform."

Chapter 13

Although stiff and sore, Buck awoke in surprisingly good spirits, feeling lucky to be alive. Beauty was awake. When he raised his head, she licked his face and demanded a hug.

"You saved my life big girl. You look as stiff and sore as I am."

The blankets were warm. He'd never known sleeping on the ground could be so comfortable. Quite naked, he was looking around for something to wear when Kristy appeared through the flap, doing a double-take when she saw him.

"Oh my God! I didn't realize last night how badly you are scratched and bruised."

"I'm lucky to be alive, and wouldn't be if it weren't for Beauty. I wouldn't look so bad if I had some clothes to wear.

"Don't worry, Cowboy. We won't make you walk around exposed all day, though I wouldn't mind." She handed him shirt and jeans, both new. "Esme threw away your filthy clothes."

"Just my size. How did you manage?"

"Don't get the big head. We have several stores in Lykaia. I know about how tall you are and we used your belt to determine your waist size."

Kristy handed him his belt and he worked it through the jean loops. He was tucking in his shirt when Esme entered the teepee.

"You look good. My therapy must have helped."

"Best I ever had. In fact, I could use a little more."

Kristy grinned. "Me too."

Esme put a hand up. "Buck has other things he needs to do right now."

"Great, I don't even have my boots."

"You'll have to wear moccasins. I sent out a patrol to Skeleton Creek this morning. They found your wallet and cell phone but not your other boot."

When Kristy stepped outside, he glanced at the missed messages on his phone.

"Better call Clayton. I'm sure he's wondering what happened to me."

"Don't tell him about the panther."

Buck started to say something but thought better of it. Clayton answered on the first ring.

"Where the hell are you? I had the boys out all night. They found the ATV and one of your boots. I thought you were dead."

"A little mishap. I'd have called sooner but I misplaced my phone."

"Where are you now?"

"Lykaia. Can you send someone to get me?"

"Sheriff Hagen's already on the way. I'll give him a call."

"Still have a job?" Esme asked when he put the phone in his pocket.

"Clayton's too much of a control freak to fire me before wringing out every last drop of information. Why didn't you want me to tell him about the panther?"

"I can't explain just yet. Please just trust me for now."

Kristy reentered the teepee before he could question Esme further. "It was Lana. The Sheriff is here and wants to see you."

Buck grinned. "That was fast."
***

One of the Lykaia vehicles waited for them outside the teepee and Buck and Kristy climbed into the back. The two compound cops drove them to the front of the Lykaia general headquarters where they found Lana and Sheriff Hagen. He cast a disbelieving glance at Buck's moccasins, the scratches on his face and neck, and then motioned him to get in his squad car.

"Want to tell me what happened last night?" he said as they drove out the front gate.

Buck shook his head. "I'm not sure I know myself."

"Uh huh."

He knew the young cowboy well enough to realize he probably had a good reason for his silence. It didn't stop him from asking.

Pressed for details, Buck said, "I'm on to something but I don't have a firm handle just yet."

"At least give me a hint."

Buck told him about the oil lease, withholding what he now knew about Garth and Roy Dunlap, and glossing over, in deference to Esme, the panther attack. Sheriff Hagen didn't miss a word.

"What have you got going with the people in the commune?"

"I told you. They asked me to help them catch the intruder and I'm doing it, with Clayton's blessing."

"I don't mind you working both sides of the fence, but just don't try it with me."

"You have my word."

"At least let me provide a little backup."

Sheriff Hagen grinned and shook his head when Buck said, "Not just yet. If I get in a bind, you'll be the first person I call."
***

Sheriff Hagen dropped him off at the front gate of Clayton's ranch. Two cowhands escorted him, still

119

carrying his lone boot under his arm, to the veranda. Clayton wasn't alone, KK standing behind him, massaging his shoulders. Buck's mouth opened when he saw her skimpy baby-doll nightie, the transparent garment doing little to cloak her marvelous body. She smiled when she saw him, hurried over and gave him a wiggly hug, and then touched the long scratch on his face.

"We've been so worried about you."

Buck glanced at Clayton and instantly knew KK was using him to elicit a little jealousy from her rich lover. By his pained expression, he realized she had scored a direct hit. She let go of him when Clayton tossed him his other boot.

"You look like you got the worst end of a cat fight. Tell me just where the hell you've been."

Buck glanced at KK, her cagey grin reminding him of the very reason they had broken up. She was a tease, and he finally grew weary of her playing him like a fiddle, sometimes second fiddle. He wrestled on his boots as Clayton waited for an explanation.

After telling a doctored version of what had happened, he saw little reason to hamper his investigation by ratting on foreman Garth, and business partner Roy Dunlap. It didn't matter because his abbreviated story seemed to satisfy Clayton. He rang for Maria to bring him a refill on his whiskey. Buck could see when she brought it KK's skimpy attire appalled her. Clayton didn't seem to notice.

"I'm leaving for Kansas City in a few days. Roy and me are going to a cattle auction."

And probably a half-dozen topless joints, Buck thought. When he glanced at KK, she smiled, winked at him, and then disappeared into the bedroom.

Clayton walked him to his Navigator. "How close are you to getting me some answers?"

"Don't shoot me, Boss. I'm working fast as I can."

"I know," Clayton said, giving Buck's shoulder a

fatherly tap "What am I going to do with KK?"

"I don't have a clue what you're talking about."

"Yes you do. You saw her, parading around half-naked. The hands are all talking behind my back and Maria will hardly look me in the eye."

"KK's a lot of woman. You knew it when you took up with her."

"You think she's too much woman for me?"

Buck grinned. "I don't know about you, but she was more than a handful for me. I finally had to call calf rope."

Clayton smiled as Buck cranked the Navigator's engine. He nodded and started to put the vehicle into gear but Clayton raised a hand.

"Yes Sir?"

"I'd like to take the lady at the commune up on her offer to visit the place."

"When would you like to go?"

Clayton glanced at his Rolex."How about right now?"

Chapter 14

Buck dialed Lana, explaining when she answered that Clayton wanted to take the tour of Lykaia she had offered.

"When would he like to come?"

"Right now."

"Not much notice."

"Mr. O'Meara is a man of action."

"Bring him over. I'll personally escort him."

Clayton listened to the one-sided conversation, smiling when Buck nodded.

"We're on. How long will it take you to get ready?"

"I was born ready," he said with a wolfish grin. "Let me get my hat."

Like Buck, and almost every other cowboy on the ranch, Clayton usually wore a Stetson. They both looked sharp in their pressed Levi's and Western-cut shirts, and Buck felt better wearing his favorite boots again instead of the moccasins. Clayton's big silver belt buckle bore the shape of a rodeo bull and accented a slender waistline for a man his age.

"Which vehicle?" Buck asked.

"You drive. I'm just along for the ride. How far is it?"

"As the crow flies, the compound is beyond

Skeleton Creek, just over the hill. Since we don't have wings, it's a little more round-about getting there."

"I'm not going to have any surprises, am I?"

Buck grinned. "Surprises, hell, I'm not sure you'll believe your eyes."

"Now you've piqued my interest."

"I won't spoil it for you. You'll see for yourself soon enough."

The two familiar female guards met them at the front gate, escorting them in their electric vehicle to the main business area. Clayton drank in the windmills and half-buried structures they drove past. The two women let them out at the front door of the Administration Building.

"Lana is expecting you."

"Thanks," Buck said as he and Clayton climbed out of the vehicle.

Clayton followed Buck down the short flight of stairs and past the young lady sitting at the control desk who simply smiled and waved them toward Lana's office. Clayton apparently expected a stodgy old woman instead of a beautiful red haired beauty with eyes a color of pale blue few humans have. When she turned and smiled, he yanked off his hat, slicked his silver hair and moustache with a quick swipe of his big hand, and then returned her smile with one of his own.

"I am Lana, Chief Administrator of Lykaia. You must be Mr. O'Meara."

"Clayton, call me Clayton," he said, taking her hand and holding it a bit too long.

Clayton was tall and unused to looking into the eyes of a woman fully six-feet tall herself.

"I'm sorry we haven't met before now," she said.

"If I had known such a gorgeous woman was running the place, I would have stopped by long ago."

Lana didn't blush at Clayton's blatant come-on. Having known her effect on men for many years, as Buck saw it, anything less would likely have disappointed her. Instead, she shot back with a compliment of her own.

"If I had known what a good-looking man owned the ranch next to us, I would have visited you first."

"I like you," he said. "You have a certain quality I can't quite describe."

They both laughed when she said, "Balls?"

"Buck told me a little about this place. I'm curious to have a look around."

"This place is Lykaia. It's probably quite different from anywhere else you have ever visited, and I don't think you'll be disappointed."

Clayton grabbed her hand again. "After meeting you, nothing else I see will disappoint me. I am already enchanted."

"Clayton, you are full of it," she said with a smile, wresting her hand away from his grasp and giving him a playful slap across the cheek.

Buck watched in amazement, thinking they might rip off each other's clothes any minute and go at it on the floor. They refrained themselves, but both smiled as they left the office and walked upstairs. Kristy was waiting for them and her own smile turned to a pout when she touched the long scratch on Buck's face and neck. Lana and Clayton didn't notice as she led him to an electric vehicle with no top or sides.

"Sit in back with me," Lana said. "Kristy will drive us and Buck can sit up front with her."

"It will be my pleasure," Clayton said, climbing in and not missing the abundant show of long legs as she hiked her already short skirt to step up into the vehicle.

There are no mountains in Logan County, but it isn't flat. Changes in elevation of a hundred-feet or more are common. Buck got his own first look at some of the area as they drove away from the administration buildings.

"Much of Lykaia is below ground. We have an extensive complex of tunnels which join offices, private residences, restaurants and recreational facilities. We generate the energy it takes to run our community using wind, solar, or other green means. We have a sophisticated grid unduplicated any place on earth."

"Interesting," Clayton said. "What do you do when the wind isn't blowing?"

"I detect skepticism in your voice."

"I'm in the oil business. I know of no other way to produce all the energy the world needs except by the use of fossil fuels."

"Then maybe you should open your eyes and learn a few things. Enough wind exists to supply all the energy the world will ever need. You just have to know how to harness it."

"But at what price?" he asked.

"Can you put a price on the quality of life?"

"No, but I don't think anyone wants to live without heat in the winter and air conditioning in the summer, especially here in Oklahoma."

"We have heat and air, and even indoor plumbing but we don't pollute. Look around," Lana said, pointing from one side of the vehicle to the other. "We have created a virtual Eden here."

Clayton grinned. "There must be a snake around someplace."

Crossing her arms tightly and pointing her knees away from him, she said, "I'm not talking to you anymore."

"Oh, come on now. I was only pulling your leg." Lana had to smile and shake her head when he added, "At least I'd like to pull your leg."

Lana and Clayton continued to banter like love-struck teens as Kristy drove them around Lykaia. They passed an outdoor swimming pool landscaped and designed to emulate a south Pacific lagoon. Clayton grew silent and his eyes larger when he noticed many of the female swimmers and loungers were either nude or at least partially so.

"We also have indoor and outdoor tennis courts and a nine-hole golf course. Do you golf?"

"Some of my friends consider me pretty damn good."

"Fine because I don't like playing people I can easily trounce."

"I wouldn't want to take advantage of you. You don't know it but I had a golf scholarship at Oklahoma State."

"So did I, but mine was at OU."

It was Clayton's turn to fold his arms. "I might have known. I've never met anyone from OU yet who didn't think they could beat anyone at anything."

"You find something wrong with that?"

"No, and I'm going to love whipping your gorgeous ass in golf."

"You're on, big boy. Care to put a little money where your mouth is?"

"You bet I do. I've never had a woman beat me at golf, much less a Sooner."

"Well I've never had a man beat me at golf, especially an Aggie," she said, using a nickname for Oklahoma State graduates.

Kristy stopped the electric vehicle at the top of a hill overlooking the projecting roof of an underground building. A huge satellite dish sat mounted on the roof, along with a large telescope.

"This is our science laboratory. High-speed computers connect us with similar facilities around the world. We even exchange information with NASA."

"I haven't seen any livestock," Clayton said.

"We raise catfish in underground ponds and are big into hydroponics. We grow fruit and vegetables year round and trade for what meat and dairy products we consume."

"I'll admit your landscaping impresses me, as do your buildings. Who is your architect?"

"All our work is done in-house. We have scientists,

artists, musicians and excellent chefs living here. Lykaia encourages creativity and basks in the wealth created by our highly intelligent populace."

Clayton stared in awe. "Who supports this place?"

"We trade stocks and commodities on the world market and have our fingers in lots of financial pies. We run our own bank and lend money to women all over the world."

Kristy drove past the row of windmills and Lykaia's solar generation plant, neither Lana nor Clayton missing a beat in the back seat.

"You said you have indoor plumbing. Do you use septic tanks?"

"Hardly. We have a sewage reclamation plant which returns most of the water back to the earth in a pristine form. We use the solid waste for energy generation, compost and fertilizer. An improvement we devised on a technique developed by NASA for use on the space station."

"Impressive."

They soon reached the edge of Lykaia's property on a hill looking south. Kristy stopped the vehicle, pointing out Clayton's ranch in the distance. The setting sun cast a warm glow on brown buildings with rooftops the color of teal, evoking the look of distant gemstones.

"There is much more to see underground. Are you still interested?"

"I wouldn't miss it for the world," Clayton said. "Lead the way. I'm a willing follower."

Kristy turned the vehicle around but not in the direction from where they had come. Instead, she followed the rustic wooden fence line around the perimeter. They passed the pond where Buck and the others had taken a dip following the night of revelry. They also passed the thick stand of trees familiar to Buck because of the location of Esme's teepee. A woman in uniform met them at the door of the administration building and drove away in the vehicle.

Kristy and Buck lagged behind as Clayton followed Lana down the long tunnel. Squeezing his hand, she kissed his cheek. Clayton and Lana didn't notice, too intent on each other and the cool lights illuminating the tunnel. Lana commented about the lighting before Clayton had a chance to ask.

"It's like the illumination created by light-emitting diodes. It uses very little energy and results in almost no heat loss. It is lighting at its most efficient."

"Interesting, and the temperature seems perfect. How do you maintain it at such a constant level?"

"We have a central control point which monitors temperature and energy usage in every building."

When they reached the Tiers Restaurant, a smiling hostess escorted them to Lana's table.

"I'll have a double martini," she said. "Clayton?"

"I thought you'd never ask. Jack Daniel's, neat, and make it a double."

The usual string quartet played in the background, accompanied by a woman with a wonderful voice singing an Italian aria. Clayton seemed enthralled as he downed his whiskey and motioned a passing waitress for another.

"The acoustics are marvelous and the aroma coming from the kitchen makes me remember I missed lunch."

"You won't miss dinner. We don't have a menu here. We'll have the meal of the evening and I promise you won't be disappointed."

"I've yet to be disappointed by anything," he said, his voice becoming mellow as he sipped his whiskey. She grinned, not answering when he added, "What else do you promise?"

Kristy and Buck held hands under the table, listening to Clayton and Lana's conversation as they ate their Santa Fe-style salmon enchiladas. Clayton was still smiling when they finished and moved to a dark bar offsetting the dining area. They had the secluded spot to themselves, except for the friendly bartender who seemed to know Lana's importance and treated her accordingly. Lana's significant other soon joined them.

"I'm Sara," the small blonde woman said, shaking Clayton's hand.

"Charmed," he said.

Feeling the effect of Lykaia's whiskey, he kissed her hand, unsure or not caring what her appearance meant. Sara seemed to sense that Clayton was an important guest. Buck and Kristy moved down a stool to allow her to sit beside Lana. Clayton and Lana's lively conversation continued, joined now by Sara's succinct comments and wry sense of humor. None of them noticed when Kristy and Buck moved away to a dark booth.

"Are you okay?" she asked, again caressing the claw mark on his face.

"Beauty took the brunt of the panther's attack. She's the one we should worry about."

Kristy smiled. "She's up and walking. Esme says she'll be good as new in a week or so. Can we sneak out of here?"

It was Buck's turn to smile. "With my two bosses getting snockered together at the bar, I don't think so."

"The way they are arguing, you would think they are an old married couple."

"Except both of them are smiling and Clayton has his hand on Lana's knee. I hope Sara doesn't cold cock him."

"She likes it. Clayton is getting Lana hot and Sara knows she will be the recipient of her heat later on tonight."

"You are getting me hot talking about it."

Kristy squeezed his hand. "We can do something about it if you can get us out of here."

"I'll see what I can do," he said, returning to the

bar. "You ready?"

Clayton glanced at Buck, shaking his head. "It's still early."

"It's after ten. We've been here all day and most of the night already."

"Lana and I will see he gets home," Sara said.

Buck looked at Clayton for an acknowledgment. The nod he got spoke volumes. He returned to the booth where Kristy waited.

"Well?"

Buck grabbed her hand again and helped her to her feet, leading her back to the LED-lighted hallway.

"I think someone along with Sara is going to feel Lana's heat tonight. Let's go build a fire of our own."

Chapter 15

Buck reflected on his time with KK as he stopped by Sunset Farms the next morning to thank Hector once again for covering for him. Relationships come and go, and after time had passed following a break-up, he had a way of remembering the good things and forgetting the reasons for the split. Seeing KK half-dressed on Clayton's veranda reminded him of the primary reason they had finally parted company. She had the body of a runway model and the face of a movie star. Trouble was, she knew it and played her advantage to the hilt.

Buck had all but forgotten the fights and arguments he'd had while dating her. Once, an angry cowboy had approached him on the dance floor of one of their favorite clubs. Without Buck knowing, the man had been buying drinks for KK all night. He intended to take her home with him, even if he had to fight Buck to do it.

Security guards, friends of his, had kicked the man out of the club, remedying the problem for him. KK acted the innocent angel and he didn't learn until a few days later the reason for the altercation. Similar incidents often occurred during the short time he had dated her.

On the way to Crescent Oil, he called Trey.

"How about lunch?"

"You buying?"

"Don't I always?"

"No, but if you are, let's make it Nick's. They have the best jalapeno burgers in town."

"You got it," Buck said. "See you in an hour."

Sandy flashed him a pretty grin when he entered the ornate front doors of Crescent Oil.

"Hey, Cowboy, we missed you around here. Where you been?"

"Out of town, but I'm back now. Seen Georgia?"

"Off for the day, running errands for Roy. Something I can help you with?"

Buck grinned. "There are plenty of things you could help me with, but you're dating Ty."

It was Susie's turn to grin. "Georgia will be at Nick's tonight."

"How do you know?"

"Because Roy's in Kansas City with Clayton."

"Then maybe I'll see you both there later on."

Sandy blew him a kiss as he headed down the hall to his office. He liked their sexually charged teasing and knew Sandy also did, even if there was meager chance any meaningful relationship would ever come of it.

Buck checked his inbox and laptop for messages and email. No one except Sandy had seen him arrive. Finishing what he needed to do, he headed downstairs to Nick's. Trey had beaten him there and already taken a table in a darkened corner.

"What's up, Cowboy?" he asked as Buck grabbed a chair.

Buck told him about Lykaia, omitting details of the revel and his nights with Esme and Kristy. He also told him about his adventure on the ATV. When he finished his story, he spread the crumpled topo map on the table in front of them, cocking a lamp to provide a little light in the dim restaurant.

"The reason we found Clayton's dead cow on the north side of Skeleton Creek is because the rustlers herded it there. It somehow got cut loose from the others, was tracked down and killed by the panther."

"That cat is a man-eater. We need to get some hunters out there and kill it."

"I promised Esme I wouldn't do that."

Trey looked straight into his eyes. "You know something, don't you?"

"The rustling, murder and intrusion at the compound all happened practically simultaneously. Garth Dunlap's map marked the likely spot where the rustler's got Clayton's cows out of the fence."

"Roy Dunlap's brother?"

Buck nodded. "My guess is he and Johnny Crabtree were involved in the actual rustling."

"Like I said before, there were probably three rustlcrs since Crabtree sold three cows at the auction, one cow for each of them. They stole the cattle for someone else but cut out three to sell for themselves and split the money. Sort of like a little extra bonus."

"And one of the cows they sold was Clayton's new breed."

"That's right," Trey said. "Most of the cows they rustled were probably the special ones. I'm thinking they intentionally took three regular cows to sell for their own account."

"And one of those got taken by the panther."

"So they had to sell one of the special cows," Trey said.

"They herded them north from Clayton's ranch, then down into Skeleton Creek," he said, pointing to a spot on the topo map. "They parked their cattle trailer at the oil lease, a lease owned by Crescent Oil. This implicates Roy Dunlap, or at least someone else who had access to entry into the well. Maybe they trucked the cattle up this lease-line road to the little settlement you told me about north of Crescent."

"If so, they probably have a holding pen around somewhere."

"My thoughts exactly," Buck said.

They ate their fries and jalapeno burgers, letting the fruit of their brainstorm session ferment a bit.

"I'm going to drive up and check it out," Trey finally said.

"Whoa, partner, not without me you're not."

Trey glanced at his watch. "Okay. What's wrong with right now?"

"That'll work but let's take our vehicles to Sunset Farms. I have an old van I use for surveillance that's less suspicious than my Navigator or your red Wrangler.

***

Buck's faded brown van was twenty-five years old, its odometer long since broken. It didn't matter because he only used it occasionally. Happy to see them, Pard bounded into the van, jumped into Buck's lap and licked his face.

"Bring him," Trey said. "He's probably a better detective than either of us."

Buck didn't argue. Illegal tinting darkened the windows and it seemed the perfect vehicle for driving through an area unnoticed. It didn't stop Trey from snickering.

"Where did you get this hunk of junk?"

"I found it parked in front of a farmhouse with a for sale sign in the window. The farmer sold it to me for a hundred bucks."

"Yeah, well I think you overpaid."

"No way. It has a monster V8 and runs like a sewing machine. I had the windows tinted and rigged the back with everything I need for spy work. Park this baby on the side of the road and nobody even notices, except maybe in Nichols Hills."

"Where we're headed ain't Nichols Hills," Trey

said, "Although it's possible there are just as many thieves there."

Nichols Hills is an exclusive community surrounded by sprawling Oklahoma City. Some of the City's richest residents live there. As Buck and Trey both knew, in a state populated early by Boomers and Sooners, much of the wealth hadn't come honestly.

Trey directed them to a section line road just north of the small town of Crescent. They turned on the rutted dirt road and headed west, crossing a creek on an old wooden bridge built in the thirties. A thick growth of blackjacks and sand plum bushes blocked the view on both sides of the creek and the half-dozen wild turkeys, drinking from a shallow pool, didn't bother hurrying away into the underbrush. Trey pointed to a narrow blacktop road as they crossed the creek. After making the turn, Buck pulled to the side of the road.

"You drive. Someone might recognize me if we get stopped." Crawling into the back, he grabbed a digital camera. "I'll take a few pics through the portholes."

Pard settled into the passenger's seat, wishing the window was open but not missing a thing.

"Good man," Trey said, giving him a friendly head rub before settling in behind the wheel and starting down the road.

They soon reached a tiny settlement made up of a few mobile homes, ramshackle buildings and cars without wheels sitting on cinder blocks. Choppers sat parked outside one of the trailers. The weather was warm, but a thin strand of smoke puffed from a pipe in the trailer's ceiling.

"Meth house," Trey said. "I'd bet good money on it."

Buck snapped several pictures and then moved to the opposite side of the van.

"Did you notice no one has a mailbox?"

Trey laughed. "Hell, I doubt they know how to read. They all have pet pit bulls in their backyards, though.

Where to from here?"

"Follow the blacktop. This road would be red clay unless there was something important on the other end of it."

Trey continued through the little development, the last mobile home soon giving way to more blackjacks and scrub brush. About two more miles down the narrow road, they located what they were looking for—a holding pen for cattle. What they also found was something neither had suspected.

"Take a look," Trey said.

Gone were the ticky-tacky mobile homes, replaced by several acres of a well run cattle operation. Steel fencing, painted fresh white, encircled a holding pen which held a hundred or more mixed breed cattle. A large barn, feeding troughs and cutting pens painted the picture of a large and expensive cattle operation.

Behind the pens, a road led up the hill to an ornate wrought iron gate and stone fence surrounding what appeared to be a palatial estate. A huge house centered a manicured and carefully landscaped lawn. Two black Cadillac limousines sat parked in front of the massive oak doorway, apparently waiting for someone inside.

"Holy shit!" Buck said.

"Do you see what I see?"

Buck had already noticed there were several different breeds present in the large holding pen.

"What do you make of it?"

"They must come from several herds. I don't know of a farm in Oklahoma which raises this many different breeds. I'm going to take some blood samples."

An armed man appeared from the barn when Trey, carrying his black bag, stepped out of the van. Dressed in jeans, worn boots and cowboy hat, the man waved his shotgun in a menacing and convincing manner.

"Who the hell are you?"

"The vet. Your people called me about a bacterial infection. I need to check out these cows and take some blood samples."

"No one told me anything about a vet," the man said, still brandishing his shotgun. "I'll have to call it in."

"Fine. I'll get started because this might take a while."

The cowboy started to say something, thought better of it, took the phone from his checkered western shirt and dialed someone. Trey was already in the pen and taking his first sample.

"My boss don't know anything about you being here," the cowboy said after closing his flip phone and returning his attention to Trey.

"Because I'm from Texas. I'm part of the operation down there and came up to help. It doesn't matter anyway. These cows are all infected and I don't have the correct vaccine with me to treat them."

Trey vaulted the fence and headed for the van before the addled cowboy could question him further. Opening the passenger door, he said, "Get the hell out of here."

Buck didn't need prompting, pulling away as soon as Trey slammed the door. Even Pard sensed the urgency.

"Do any good?" he asked as they hurried away down the road.

"I only had time to take two samples but it should be enough to tell us what we need to know."

"Then we scored a home run."

"Not quite," Trey said as they rounded a corner and found their path blocked by two pickup trucks and a half-dozen armed men.

"Let me do the talking," Trey said, getting out of the van. "What's the problem, fellas?"

"It's you that's got a problem, not us."

Greasy brown hair protruded from beneath the unshaven man's cowboy hat as he stepped forward, waving a deadly-looking automatic weapon.

Trey raised his hands. "Hey, we're all on the same side here."

"Bullshit! No one has a clue who you are, or what you're up to."

"We all work for the same people. I'm up from Texas. Drove here from Wichita Falls this morning. Check it out. I'm telling the truth."

Trey's lie was convincing, at least until the man from the barn came racing up behind them in his pickup, sliding slightly sideways as he squealed to a halt in the road.

"I just got the word. They ain't none of ours," he said, as he bounded out of the truck.

The armed cowboys raised their weapons and started toward Trey but the noise of squealing tires and acrid smell of burning rubber caused them to turn their attention to the van. Buck had jammed the vehicle into reverse, pushing the pickup behind him into the ditch with the van's over-sized rear bumper. The truck's driver was in the line of fire, likely the only reason the cowboys didn't open up on Buck. Slamming the gearshift into first, he raced toward them, tires still squealing.

The cowboys and Trey tried to scatter but before any of them had gone five feet, Buck tossed something out the window. An explosion of flashing light and ear-splitting sound knocked them to the ground. Buck and Pard sprang from the van, grabbing Trey and dragging him into the passenger seat. With the door still ajar, he wheeled the vehicle around, barely missing the pickup he had shoved into the ditch.

"What in holy hell?" Trey said, rubbing his ears and eyes. "This way's a dead end."

"You got a better idea?" Buck said as he gunned the van's big engine and raced away down the narrow blacktop.

Halfway back to the cattle pen, he wheeled the van off the road, down into the creek bed. A barely visible rutted dirt road followed the creek and Trey held on to his seat as the boxy vehicle bucked and swayed like a wild bull, waves of water splashing over the hood and windows as it plowed through the low-water crossing to the opposite side of the creek.

The path led up the hill to a treeless field where they saw the roof of an old abandoned barn in the distance. When they reached it, they found the wooden gate shut. Buck didn't bother stopping to open it, ramming the van straight through to the dirt road on the other side.

"What the hell did you explode back there?" Trey asked, still bumping the side of his head with his palm, trying to clear his ears.

"An FNDD."

"What the hell is that?"

"Flash and noise diversionary device—a stun grenade. One of my police buddies got me a few. Never know when you might need one to get out of a jam."

Trey was still rubbing his eyes and shaking his head. "Damn! I think I'm going to need a hearing aid."

Buck laughed but didn't slow down. "Sorry, Buddy. I couldn't use it on the bad guys without including you. You'll be all right in an hour or so."

"Thanks," Trey said. "Where are we going?"

"There's a back road from Crescent to Guthrie. I'm cutting cross-country until I reach it. Is this all going to be worth it?"

"If this operation is what I think it is, the blood samples will tell us plenty. Let's just hope those boys didn't get your tag number."

"You don't think this baby is tagged in my name, do you?"

Trey just moaned, leaned back in the seat and closed his eyes.

The remaining trip to Sunset Farms proved uneventful, Trey feeling better as he exited the old van and climbed into his Wrangler.

"I'm going to get my people involved in this little cattle operation we discovered. Hopefully we didn't spook them enough to start shutting down."

"And if they do?"

"There are still things we can learn. Someone owns, or is leasing that facility. We'll follow the money and it will lead us to the principals. I'll keep in touch. Meantime, stay off the road in your van."

Buck waved as Trey drove away from Sunset Farms. For the first time in several days, he performed the afternoon feeding, Pard on his heels. Then he went upstairs, took a shower and changed clothes. Georgia would be at Nick's, having a drink, and he needed to see her.

"You stay and keep an eye on LaDona and her baby. I have to go to town and they don't allow border collies in Nick's."

Chapter 16

It was dark when Buck reached the Petro Place, parked the Navigator and entered Nick's. The dimly lighted bar rocked with patrons listening to the piano player singing oldies. He found Georgia sitting alone in a booth, nursing a rum and Coke. She smiled when he slid in beside her. Scooting closer, she hugged him. Her low-cut blouse and lavender miniskirt displayed far more than breasts and nice legs, and caused him to take a deep breath.

"You look great, even with all your clothes on."

She grinned, knowing what he was getting at. "I can say the same for you. Lykaia is good for me. We all help each other. It's like the family I never had."

"But you don't live there."

"Residence isn't a requirement although I have an apartment I use sometimes."

"What is it you do for Lykaia?"

"Anything they ask me to do," she answered bluntly.

The piano player sang Neil Diamond's Sweet Caroline as many of the club's patrons joined in with him.

"I was pretty stoned at the revel but I can't forget seeing you and how hot you looked."

Georgia grinned. "You were pretty hot yourself. I tried to get your attention but I think some of the other women had dibs on you. Maybe it's time we changed all that."

The noise level in Nick's was high, lights dim. No one seemed to notice when she slipped her hand between his legs and squeezed. They were, in an instant, locked in an amorous embrace and sensual kiss, his loins burning when Ronnie brought his Wild Turkey.

They both laughed when she said, "You two get a room."

Buck managed to pull away from Georgia and sipped his whiskey until he caught his breath.

"Lana hired me to investigate the intruder. I know we talked about it but it's just now dawning on me how much you resemble KK. You are both about the same height and your hair the same color and length."

"I told you we were roomies in college and best friends. People mistake us for sisters and its fun playing the game. We usually hang together when Roy and Clayton are out of town."

"Did you know the man murdered on Clayton's ranch?"

Georgia's smile disappeared and she nodded. "Frankie Boggs. He was like a big brother to me. You remember the lingerie shows they used to have around town?"

"Maybe I heard about them."

"You went, just like every other horny oilie. Frankie and I would go for lunch. He worked for Clayton and helped me get my job with Crescent Oil."

"Did you and KK do anything with him before he was killed?"

Georgia didn't have to think about it. "We went two-stepping the very night it happened. You know Rustlers? The dance floor is gigantic."

Buck had spent many Friday nights in Rustlers, a western-themed nightspot that featured live bull riding.

"Of course I do."

"KK said she told you about our adventure with the man who works for Roy. The one with fighting dogs and a big knife."

"Jimmy Quick. You saw him at Rustler's?"

"Frankie saw him first. He wanted to say something to him but KK and I were both frightened Jimmy might hurt him, so we split."

"To another bar?"

"We were already wasted and decided to call it a night. Since Jimmy knows where I live, Frankie drove us to Logan County and dropped us at the Lykaia front gate. KK and I spent the night at my apartment."

"Did Quick follow you there?"

"I don't know. We were all a little looped and forgot about Jimmy soon as we left Rustlers."

"Maybe he waited until Frankie dropped you and KK off and then followed him back to Clayton's ranch."

Georgia thought about it a moment. "What are you getting at?"

Buck evaded the question and said instead, "I wish I knew what he looked like."

"That's easy," she said, reaching for her fancy cell phone. "I take pictures of everyone on my phone list. When they call, their picture shows up on the screen. Here he is with KK."

Buck studied the image of the handsome cowboy standing at least a foot taller than the smiling KK.

"Did you take this the night you two picked him up?"

Georgia nodded. "He likes to hang out at the Rock Bar with the bunch of degenerates who live north of Crescent."

Buck motioned Ronnie to bring him his tab. "I'm going out there."

"Not to do anything crazy, I hope. You are a big man but Jimmy is bigger."

"I just want to get a look at him."

"Leaving kind of early, aren't you Cowboy?" Ronnie said as he stood to leave.

"Got to get my beauty rest," he answered as he headed toward the door.

Georgia followed him through the crowded bar. "You're not going without me."

"He knows you and it would cause a problem. I only want to get a good look, not confront him."

"I don't care. I'm coming," she said, following him to the parking garage. "He won't bother me if I'm with you."

Buck turned her around, pointing her back toward Nick's. "As much as I'd like to take you two-stepping, you would blow my cover. I'll catch you later."

Buck was barely out of the parking lot when he called Trey Calderham.

"I didn't wake you, did I?"

Trey laughed. "Beth usually works at the restaurant until it closes and I don't go to bed until she does. What's up?"

"Just wanted to ask how you were feeling, and to see if you had anything more on the cattle operation north of Crescent."

"My ears finally stopped ringing and I only see a few spots now when I close my eyes. Other than that, I think I'll live. I got the test results of the two blood samples I took. Like we thought, the cows were from farms around here, one as far away as Seminole County."

"Which means?"

"The operation is well organized. The cattle in the holding pen have one thing in common; they are all excellent breeding stock. We don't usually see this quality of cattle at the livestock sales. And Buck, the person who owns the ranch is Roy Dunlap."

"Are you kidding me?"

"Cattle rustling is something I don't kid about. So

what are you up to?"

"I'm on my way to the Rock Bar to check out the place."

"It's a hangout for the gang north of Crescent. Better wait and let me join you."

"No thanks."

What'll you do if one of those goons recognizes you?"

"I barely got out of the van, but you did. That's why I need to do this alone."

"Not a good idea."

"Maybe not, but it's the best one I have," he said, saying goodbye before Trey could protest further.

Leaving Nick's, he followed back roads to the Rock Bar, a local landmark that had received its name from its red sandstone façade. It was a place frequented by both the rich and famous, and the locals loved it. Buck pulled into the parking lot beside a midnight blue Dodge pickup. The vanity tag on the expensive truck bore only a large Q. There was either more money in dog and chicken fighting then Buck knew about, or else Jimmy Quick was into other things.

The parking lot brimmed with every imaginable vehicle, from expensive BMWs and Mercedes to old pickup trucks. Western swing music streamed from an open back door, Friday night and payday the reason for the large crowd. Located far enough from Guthrie, the rustic bar didn't worry about fire ordinances or noise levels. People crowded outside on the large wooden deck, lighted with Japanese lanterns, overlooking the parking lot. Buck waded through the jean and boot-clad young men and women, all clutching cold beers.

Patrons inside stood shoulder-to-shoulder, either at the stained wooden bar, or watching dancers two stepping to the music of a live, loud band. Those lucky enough to have tables or booths ignored the masses pressing close to them.

"What'll you have?" the young bartender with slicked-down dark hair asked.

"Coors, in a bottle if you have it."

"The best way to drink it," he said, retrieving an icy Coors from the cooler beneath the counter. "I'm Jacob. I didn't catch your name."

"James," Buck said, giving him his real first name. "You have a nice crowd here tonight."

"Lots of pretty girls and even more horny Friday night cowboys."

Buck slammed his beer, sat the bottle on the polished countertop and nodded for another. Noise in the building lessened as the band finished its last song before taking a break. An attractive cowgirl, decked out in frayed jean shorts, boots, pink crop top and cowboy hat, dropped a glass. When it shattered on the hardwood floor, applause and laughter erupted. Jacob moved away to pour a beer for another customer.

With his back against the bar, Buck scanned the crowd. It didn't take him long to spot Jimmy Quick, taller than most of the others in the packed room. He was talking to two cowboys. With the band on break, many of the drinkers and dancers went outside to smoke and enjoy the mild night. The two men with Quick went with them, but not before one of them pointed at Buck. He knew something was up because Quick soon sidled up beside him.

"I'm Jimmy," he said, not offering to shake Buck's hand. "I haven't seen you in here before."

Buck nodded and smiled. "I'm James and I haven't been in lately."

Jimmy was tall, probably six-five or six. The muscles in his broad shoulders and barrel chest rippled through the fabric of his sky blue Western shirt, opulently decorated with epaulets and buckskin laces. Like Jacob, he had dark hair protruding from beneath his expensive cowboy hat.

Like practically every person in the place, he wore

jeans. Unlike most of the other patrons, his weren't Levi's or Wrangler's, but freshly pressed designer jeans. His hand-tooled exotic animal skin boots would cost most men a month's wages. They complemented his expensive Rolex and huge diamond pinkie ring. Jimmy didn't skimp at the dentist's office either, flashing a set of freshly whitened teeth which looked almost too perfect.

A pretty woman with long bleached hair beneath her fancy Stetson stumbled through the crowd and grabbed his arm. Like Jimmy's diamond ring and gold Rolex, she was a flashy ornament. He didn't bother introducing her and from her inane grin, Buck could tell she was either too soused or stoned to care. He had garnered Jimmy's attention and the big cowboy apparently didn't want the woman around while he talked to him. Pulling a wad of hundreds from his jeans, he handed a bill to her.

"It's too quiet in here. Go put some money in the jukebox."

Jimmy patted her butt, earning him a smile and suggestive wiggle as she took the Bennie and stumbled away through the crowd.

Buck didn't comment when Jimmy said, "She's a great piece of ass but dumb as a stump."

He was thinking seriously about making an early exit when Quick's two friends joined them. One of them was Johnny Crabtree, and Buck hoped he didn't remember him from Clayton's ranch.

"This is Johnny and Shorty. What's your name again?"

"James Tee," Buck said.

Johnny looked at him closely. "I know you from someplace.

"Not that I can remember."

"Where do you work?"

They all turned at once when an obviously inebriated voice said, "He's Clayton O'Meara's right hand man. Isn't he gorgeous?"

Someone from the crowded dance floor joined them and edged in between Buck and Jimmy. The stunning woman put her arms around his neck and kissed him passionately. It was KK.

Chapter 17

"What a lucky girl I am, finding the two best looking men in Oklahoma waiting together at the bar for me. Any chance of a three-way?"

KK was the last person he expected to see and his heart started to race. From Jimmy's expression, he was also surprised to see her.

"How do you know James?"

"I was only eighteen the first time he got into my pants, and everyone I know calls him Buck."

Buck just grinned and shook his head. KK was drunk and had already blown his cover. Grabbing her hand, he said, "I need to get her home. We'll talk again later."

Johnny Crabtree clamped down on his shoulder and said, "What's your hurry?"

"Sounds like we need to do some talking now," Quick said. "Let's take a walk outside."

Buck glanced behind him, wondering if he and KK could get through the crowd and out the door before a fight broke out.

They might have made it except Jimmy's blonde girlfriend returned from the jukebox. Frowning when she saw KK, she grabbed the front of her blouse, ripping it until it gaped open, the buttons gone. She didn't leave it at that, dealing KK's face a backhanded slap that snapped her head back.

Blood streamed from the corner of KK's mouth, but no tears appeared in her eyes. She returned the favor, but with her fist clenched tightly. The blow sent Jimmy's girlfriend backwards into the bar. It wasn't a knockout punch and only infuriated her. After wiggling her chin to assure herself it wasn't broken, she launched into KK, rolling her to the dirty wooden dance floor.

"Cat fight!" someone yelled, as the music stopped and the crowd closed around the two women, wrestling and clawing on the floor.

Jimmy forgot about Buck and turned his attention to the fight. Grabbing arms and shoulders, he shoved a half-dozen verbose fight observers out of his way. When he made it to the center of the human ring, he grabbed the woman's arm and yanked her to her feet.

"You crazy bitch," he said as he popped her head back with a vicious backhand.

When Buck shoved his way to the center of activity, KK nailed him with a fist in the face as he tried to help her off the floor. He was reeling from the punch when Jimmy wheeled him around and took a roundhouse swing at him. Buck ducked, but caught a violent knuckle to the chin. Realizing Jimmy was too big to fight straight up, he dived for his knees and rolled him to the floor. A champion wrestler in high school, he knew the dirty bar floor was his element. His ploy almost succeeded. He was getting the best of the much larger man when someone kicked him in the side.

The fight was on, fists swinging and objects thrown. Jimmy was squeezing his neck, another man pummeling him when a gunshot sounded, knocking out the lights. Darkness engulfed the participants in the barroom brawl. The shooter nailed Jimmy with the butt of the pistol and then got into it with the other cowboy. Buck scooted backwards, pivoting wildly, looking for KK. He found her directly behind him, into it again with the blonde woman. Grabbing her arm, he pulled her through the riotous crowd and out the back door.

"I know you're having fun but I think those three cowboys want to kill me. Let's get the hell out of here. And hey, you pack a hell of a punch," he said as they raced away from the melee.

KK's blouse was in shreds and she grinned as she sat in the front seat of the Navigator, her arms crossed tightly.

"That was fun," she said. "Where are you taking me?"

"To Clayton's."

"Not the way I look. Your place."

"No way. You think I'm crazy? Clayton would kill me."

"Only if you tell him. I'm damn sure not."

Buck had dealt with the headstrong KK more than once and knew she wasn't going to take no for an answer. Finally squealing into Sunset Farms, he parked the car in front of the barn and led her upstairs to his suite.

"You never brought me here before," she said when he turned on the lights.

"Because Clayton's ex is as jealous as he is. Lucky for us, she's in Scotland."

"Lucky for me," she said, putting her arms around him and pulling close.

"I can't do this, KK. I have loyalty to Clayton and you are his woman now."

"You and your silly code of honor. I need a shower. At least point me in the direction of your bathroom."

"Through that door," he said.

KK returned with wet hair and only a damp towel concealing her nudity.

"Do you have something I can wear, or would you prefer me totally naked?"

Buck grinned and shook his head, handing her an extra-large orange tee shirt which said OSU Cowboys.

KK took the soft cotton garment. "You and your precious team. When are you going to get a clue OU not only plays the best football in Oklahoma, but anywhere."

"I'd advise you not to share your opinion with Clayton. You can have the bed. I'll sleep on the couch after I take a shower."

He slipped into the bathroom and let hot water pour over his head and shoulders. After the stressful day, it felt like heaven. He luxuriated in the steamy stall when soft breasts pressed against his spine.

"You know we can't do this," he said, protesting.

KK didn't answer, and Buck's resolve soon disappeared, along with soapy water swirling down the drain.

***

Buck awoke with his arms around a familiar, very warm female body, feeling wonderful, even if he didn't think very highly of himself. When he got up and looked in the mirror, he realized he had a black eye. His chin also ached, as did his ribs where someone had kicked him. KK was still asleep when he returned from feeding Pard and the horses.

He shook her shoulder. "Gonna sleep all day?"

"What I wouldn't mind doing all day doesn't involve sleeping."

"My guilt meter is already pegged. I can't handle anymore for a day or two. Besides, Clayton is probably on his way home from Kansas City."

"You asshole, you sound like my Mother."

"Are you trying to break up with Clayton?"

"No way. I love him."

"Like a father?"

"I have a father. I love him like a man."

Irritated by his haranguing, she got out of bed and strolled naked to the bathroom, giving him an unobstructed view of her gorgeous rear end. When she returned, she had on one of his robes. He grinned, but not so she could see him, when he saw she also had a black eye.

"I'm not sure who got the worst of the fight last night, you or me."

KK didn't laugh. "It's not funny. What am I going to tell Clayton?"

"Tell him you missed him so much you drove to your Mom's in Tulsa, and she had missed you so much you decided to stay a few days."

"You are good," KK said. "I haven't seen Mom in three months and this is as good a time as any."

"How will you explain the black eye and bruises?"

She smiled for the first time. "I never lie to my mom. You wouldn't happen to have a blouse around would you? Some wildcat ripped mine to shreds."

Buck didn't but LaDona did. She took KK under her wing, doctoring her scratches and applying makeup to mask the black eye. They were soon on their way back to the Rock Bar to retrieve her white Mercedes.

KK gazed out of her open window with pleading eyes as she prepared to head to Tulsa. "You promise you'll never mention a word of this to Clayton?"

"I don't remember a thing."

Grinning, she waved to him as she tooled away. Buck watched her go before heading north to the brick-paved streets of Guthrie. The first territorial capital of Oklahoma was one of the starting points for the land run of 1889. It grew from nothing to a town with a population of ten thousand people in less than half a day. He parked the Navigator in front of the new police station.

The old Logan County Jail was little more than a medieval dungeon. Located below the County courthouse, it was dilapidated and dangerous. Prisoners hated the old facility to the extent jailbreaks and escape attempts had become endemic. Hagen had somehow found the money to change the scenario. The new Logan County Jail, a state-of-the-art facility and model for the entire United States, even housed Federal prisoners.

Sheriff Hagen had not stopped with the jail, reaching out to the surrounding communities, offering help. Langston, a mostly black college community not far away, never had much of a law force. Hagen began assisting with their problems, and provided much needed aid when a tornado caused havoc in the tiny college town. The cute worker behind the bulletproof window of the dispatch office waved at Buck and buzzed him into the hall leading to administration, Hagen shaking his head when he entered his door without knocking.

"The prodigal son returns. Nice black eye."

"You should see the other guy," Buck said.

Buck was neither Hagen's son, nor Hagen Buck's dad. Raised in foster homes, he never knew his real father. Sheriff Hagen was married but had no children of his own and they both enjoyed the illusion of being father and son.

"You owe me. Carol was feeling frisky for the first time in a month and she didn't appreciate me leaving her alone to bail your butt out of a crack."

If Sheriff Hagen was Buck's surrogate dad, his wife Carol was his mom. He had eaten more Sunday dinners at her table than any place else he could think of, and it was Carol he always called when he needed advice about women.

"You were at the Rock Bar last night?"

"Trey called and warned me there might be trouble. Good thing he did because we had to break up a near riot when we got there. You didn't have anything to do with starting it, did you?"

"I left early."

"Uh huh! We arrested a dozen people." Hagen pivoted his chair to the pot behind him and poured two cups of black coffee, handing one to Buck. "A stray bullet put your buddy Trey in the hospital."

The grin on Buck's face disappeared. "Trey was there?"

"He took a slug in the chest. He's at St. Clemmon's in critical condition."

"Who shot him?"

"Half the people in the place were packing. We found most of the weapons under the tables and in the parking lot where their owners tossed them when we showed up."

"Thanks, Sheriff. If I were you, I'd send Carol a dozen roses."

"Yeah, and if I were you, I'd put on a pair of sunglasses to cover that shiner. Hey, call tomorrow and remind me about the roses."

***

St. Clemmon's Hospital is in the northwest part of Oklahoma City and Buck had spent time there in the emergency room more than once. After learning Trey's location, he followed the halls to Intensive Care where he found Beth holding Trey's hand, IV's and medical instruments attached to his arms with tubes and wires. She backed away when he walked around the bed to hug her.

"How is he?"

"Alive, no thanks to you."

"I never planned for this to happen."

"Maybe that's your problem."

Buck let the remark pass, asking instead, "Is there anything I can do?"

Beth's anger disappeared. Putting her arms around him, she squeezed herself to his chest and sobbed.

"Oh Buck, I'm so frightened."

Her words aroused Trey from his drug-induced stupor. "I'm in the hospital one minute and you've already got your hands on my girl."

155

Buck squeezed his shoulder. "I know we're friends, but you didn't have to take a bullet for me."

"If I hadn't, you probably wouldn't have a head. Your good buddy was about to chop it off with his big knife."

"I should have known it was you who shot out the lights and nailed Jimmy Quick. If you count fishing me out of Guthrie Lake, this makes the second time you saved my life."

"Third counting Pandora's," Trey said, managing a weak smile. "Can you take Beth to get something to eat? She hasn't left the room since I got here."

"You trust me with her?"

"No way, Cowboy, but I trust her."

Trey's eyes closed when Buck and Beth left the hospital room, gently shutting the door behind them. They were only a few steps down the hall when Beth's eyes began tearing.

"The Doctor thinks he will pull through but there are so many things which still can happen."

Buck led her to the elevator and then down a narrow hallway to the cafeteria. Institutional food is never wonderful, but the fare at St. Clemmon's was tolerable. Buck followed her through the line, making sure she filled her plate. After an amorous night with KK he was famished, piling his own plate with catfish fillets and French fries.

"Trey will be fine," he said between bites. "He was my best friend growing up but we came to our share of blows. Believe me when I tell you, there's not a tougher hombre in Oklahoma."

Beth smiled for the first time. "Trey is the man of my dreams and I would die if I lost him."

"You aren't going to lose him, I promise you."

"I could kill the monster who did this to him."

She shook her head when he said, "Sheriff Hagen seems to think he caught a random bullet."

"The knife wound wasn't random."

"What knife wound?"

Beth began sobbing again. "Someone carved the letter Q into his back."

Buck managed to calm Beth again but the news about Trey's knife wound struck him like a sledgehammer to the chest. If he'd had doubts before now about who had questioned Hector and LaDona, he no longer did. It made him wonder why the Sheriff hadn't told him about Trey's deliberate disfigurement.

He and Beth had swirled cones of chocolate and vanilla ice cream before returning to the elevators. She stopped when they reached them, grasping his hand and sobbing again. Buck held her until her tears ceased.

"Trey'll finish the investigation himself when he gets out of here. Maybe you should go home and get some rest."

"I'm not going anywhere except back upstairs."

Buck watched the elevator doors close, thinking seriously about finding Jimmy Quick, taking him someplace secluded and fucking him up.

Chapter 18

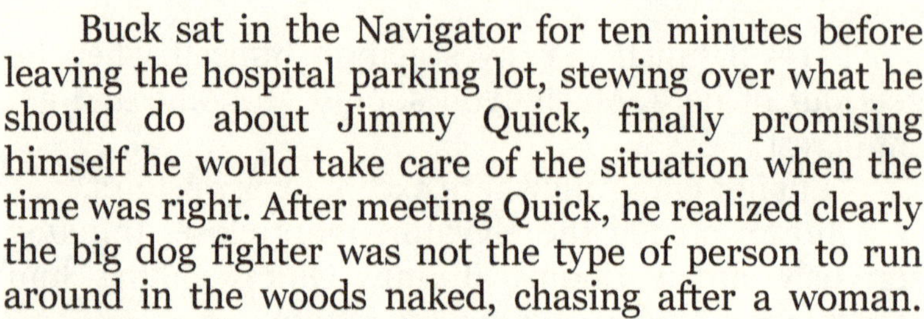

Buck sat in the Navigator for ten minutes before leaving the hospital parking lot, stewing over what he should do about Jimmy Quick, finally promising himself he would take care of the situation when the time was right. After meeting Quick, he realized clearly the big dog fighter was not the type of person to run around in the woods naked, chasing after a woman. Something else was going on at Lykaia and it didn't make a lot of sense.

Quick may have lusted after Georgia and KK, but he also had access to other women, as apparent by the blonde who had given KK the black eye. Maybe Quick was good with a knife, but it didn't mean he had killed Frankie Boggs, or cut the letter Q in Trey's back. Maybe not, but Buck no longer harbored any doubt.

***

Buck opened the moon roof on the way to Lykaia, the weather warm and a persistent breeze setting up an arboreal wave as it whistled through the trees. The two familiar Lykaia cops met him at the gate in their electric squad car and drove him to the police station.

The older of the two women simply grunted and shook her head when he said, "Nice weather today."

Ava Pruitt handed him a manila folder filled with

photos and poured him a cup of coffee. The black and whites showed a ghostly blur emanating a pallid aura. Buck could only shake his head.

"My people can deal with a human intruder, but I don't have a clue what these pictures mean. What now?"

"If it's a spirit we're dealing with, your guess is as good as mine."

Kristy entered the Constable's office as Ava and Buck wrapped up their conversation. Ava closed the manila folder and began tidying her desk.

"We're done for now, but I'll stay after it," she said.

Kristy grabbed Buck's arm when they were out the door. "Did you miss me?"

"Like crazy. Do we need to report to Lana?"

"I think Lana has already forgotten about this intruder thing."

Buck blinked. "What do you mean?"

"She told me to give you this and tell you Ava would finish the investigation."

Buck glanced at a check for three thousand dollars drawn on the Bank of Lykaia.

"All I have turned up so far is a blank, but getting fired still hurts."

Kristy grinned. "You can't get fired. You're a consultant, not a full-time employee."

"I didn't do three thousand dollars worth of work."

Buck blinked again when Kristy squeezed his hand and said, "Believe me, Lana thinks you earned every penny of it."

They continued down the dimly lit hallway, Buck stashing the check in his shirt pocket as he wondered how to interpret Kristy's cryptic remark. On the way, he told her a bit about the cattle rustling investigation.

"Trey's people are trying to trace the source of money."

"Lana can help," Kristy said. "She is connected, and not just in Oklahoma. I'll speak to her about it."

"We can't afford to compromise the investigation."

"Trust me, Lana understands security. Do you have plans for tonight?"

"Go home and turn in early."

Buck needed little persuading when Kristy smiled and said, "You'll have more fun if you stay with Esme and me."

Sunny weather had disappeared, replaced now by dark bloated clouds floating rapidly overhead. Strobe-like flashes of lightning lit the southwest skyline, followed by distant thunder. Rain began sprinkling their shoulders as he followed her down the wooded trail. As they entered Esme's teepee, the light sprinkle of rain changed abruptly into a heavy deluge.

They found Esme sitting on a colorful rug, facing the small fire which always seemed to burn inside the teepee. Beside her was Beauty. Esme had an arm around her. The poor animal was shivering, its body flinching every time thunder rumbled.

"My big brave wolf dog is a baby when it comes to thunderstorms."

Buck and Kristy joined them on the blanket, luxuriating in the warmth of the open fire. Beauty whimpered once and then changed positions, squirming to place her body into the space between Esme and Buck. Despite the raging storm, he felt secure and cozy inside the teepee. Beauty's incessant quivering abated as she drew as close to him as physically possible. Esme and Kristy both noticed.

"I'm sending Beauty to stay with you next time we have a storm," Esme said.

"I have a better idea. Next time it storms, I'll show up over here."

Kristy smiled. "I like that idea."

The storm continued for most of the night, rain falling, stopping and then starting again. Beauty didn't join Kristy, Esme and Buck in the sleeping pallet but was never far away. She was still by his side when he awoke the next day.

"Morning, Miss Beauty," he said, hugging her big neck. "Where's your mama?"

As if understanding Buck's question, she left the dim teepee, soon returning with Esme.

"I don't know how you ever get any work done, sleeping as late as you do."

Buck glanced at his old Rolex. "It's only seven."

"Some of us have been up since five."

"Maybe some of you didn't expend as much energy as I did last night."

Esme smiled. "You definitely know how to warm a girl up."

The rest of the morning included scrambled eggs wrapped in a tortilla along with a pot of black coffee Esme brewed over an open flame. By midmorning, they were naked in the hot tub. Sitting across from her in muted light of a cloudy day, Buck took pleasure in her exotic beauty and strange tattoo whose meaning he could only guess at. Wet from their soak, her long ebon hair accented dark eyes as it draped her lithe back and shoulders. Oklahoma was the original Indian Territory and even today has the largest population of Native Americans. Even so, few full-blood Indians now remain, even in Oklahoma. From her appearance, Esme could pass as a full blood Native American.

She grinned when he asked, "What tribe are you?"

"What makes you think I'm an Indian?"

"Just a guess but you do live in a teepee, cook on an open fire, and wear a breechcloth."

"Archeologists call us Mississippians."

"I never heard of that tribe."

"Because there aren't many of us left."

"How many?"

"Just me."

Buck's mouth opened but no words immediately issued forth. He finally said, "You're kidding, right?"

"I'm very serious. You've heard of the Spiro

Mounds?"

Everyone in Oklahoma knew about the Spiro Mounds. Buck had visited once while in grade school and had never forgotten the only remaining location from one of the most important Pre-Colombian archeological sites in the United States.

"I didn't know there were any Mississippians left. Where is your family from?"

Esme didn't answer and Buck realized he had overstepped his bounds when she responded coolly to his question.

"Why is it important to you?"

"I was just looking at you, thinking how drop dead gorgeous you are and wondering what sort of wonderful family heritage you must have that endowed you with such brains and beauty."

Esme smiled despite herself. "It's easy for me to recognize your heritage, Mr. Blarney Stone."

Esme pushed him away when he tried to put his arms around her.

"What?"

"There is a time and place for everything. This is neither the time nor the place, so keep your big hands to yourself."

Buck knew a rebuke when presented with one. "Sorry, the old demon testosterone was trying to take charge again."

"Oh, you mean something else controls your brain from time to time?"

"Funny."

Esme rolled her big dark eyes. "Yes, we're without clothes in the hot tub but you have seen me naked on more than one occasion. We have other things to talk about so get hold of yourself."

Esme covered her face, shook her head and moaned when she realized her verbal gaffe.

"Truce," Buck said, grinning and holding up his right hand in the universal sign of peace. "I do have a few questions for you."

Buck told her about Ava's photos.

Esme reached behind her and grabbed a pipe, a ceremonial cloud blower. After lighting it and taking a puff, she handed it to him.

"To learn the answers you seek, you must take a journey and I can not accompany you."

Chapter 19

Barefoot and dressed only in a breechcloth, Buck followed a path, Beauty by his side. They were in a forest, but unlike any forest he had ever seen, the trees surrounding them gigantic, probably never cut. There was no underbrush, or growth of vines beneath the trees, so tall and massive they blocked most of the light from the sun.

Ground fog rolled slowly across their loamy pathway, rising as high as the base of lower limbs on the massive trees. The result was a dreamlike aura made even more surreal by effervescent violet and purple light filtering through the branches. There was only silence, and when Buck spoke to Beauty, his words sounded hollow and muted, his voice resonating from somewhere deep in his lungs.

"Where are we, girl?" he asked, not feeling his lips move.

Fog swirled in rivulets around their legs as they continued along. Buck had no sense of where they were going. It didn't seem to matter; his head swam from the drug he had smoked in the pipe. Beauty seemed to know where she was going and he followed her.

He soon realized they were not alone. Giant butterflies and even larger moths fluttered with wings of iridescent green and azure through the rolling fog, their colorful appendages setting up rippling patterns of clashing colors as they parted the mist engulfing them. When they reached a barely discernible path, Beauty stopped and looked up at him.

She didn't react when he asked, "Which way, girl?"

Pulsating light emanated from the emerald wings of a creature which looked like a giant Luna moth. Beauty did not start when it fluttered for a moment directly in their path and then disappeared into the misty distance. The two travelers continued along the trail, as much subliminal as real. Buck had the sense he was floating and not walking. Perhaps he was.

They continued for an interminable time, going many miles or perhaps only a few hundred yards. It didn't matter because all sense of time, space and distance had abandoned his psyche. When they reached the intersection of two paths, Beauty sat on the ground and waited for him. Again, he realized he would have to make the decision.

As he glanced around, wondering what to do, a slight breeze began wafting away the mist. The air around him filled with a visage of light bursting forth in small explosions of color, and then disappearing like wraiths in the night. Buck glanced at Beauty again. She offered no direction for his ever-increasing feelings of doubt. The sound of a crow caused him to glance into the trees. The bird was large, its wings a luminous black which shimmered like ebon paint in a stirred can.

The crow didn't answer when Buck asked, "Which path?"

Watching it fly away, he wondered if it were a sign, telling them the path to follow. An ebony feather lost by the bird twirled slowly to earth, its quill pointing opposite the direction from where the crow had flown. Picking up the feather and putting it in his hair, Buck and Beauty took that path, soon reaching a stream.

Water appeared to flow almost like a computer

simulation, its movement created by illusions of the mind rather than actual motion. When Buck touched it, his toe ignited a burst of green and red. He and Beauty waded into the icy water, their movement sending soundless explosions of vivid color flashing around their legs.

The path widened and narrowed, and then widened again, exotic plants with colorful flowers blooming on either side. There was no sound, not even the crunch of leaves beneath their feet as they trod the path. Trees began giving way to a distant clearing. Sensing they were near their destination, Buck and Beauty picked up their pace.

Rolling fog parted as they entered a clearing abutting a large lake, its water so clear and free of ripples, he could see fish swimming just below its surface. A golden loon soared overhead, suspended almost motionless in a thermal updraft. They walked along the water's edge, sometimes following its cobbled bank, and sometimes wading in its warm shallows. Raindrops sprinkled their shoulders, evaporating as fast as it fell. The sky turned cloudy and Buck watched lightning bolts race across the darkening sky. The light show was noiseless, unaccompanied by thunder.

The soundless storm continued for what seemed a very long time when suddenly rain and lightning ceased. The sky cleared and lightened to reveal a rainbow which breached the heavens. Purple martens soared overhead, chasing invisible insects. As Buck turned a corner leading to a cove in the lake, he somehow understood they had reached their destination.

A log cabin sat near the center of the cove, wisps of smoke rising from its thatched roof. Solid limestone rose up a hundred feet behind the cabin and a lone eagle soared high above them. Buck glanced at it, and then at the winding path of colorful cobbles leading to the cabin door. When Beauty circled a spot and lay in the soft sand, Buck somehow knew he must enter the cabin alone. He did so, not bothering to knock first.

Pungent odors of herbs and burning wood met his nostrils as he eased through the creaky door, the dimly lit room revealing the outline of a man sitting on the ground beside a small fire.

"Come in my son," the man said without bothering to turn around. "Join me by the flame."

Buck sat on the ground beside him and warmed his hands. You knew I was coming?"

The man was a very old Indian, his hair snowy white, as were his eyebrows, his prominent brow crowning a regal Aztec nose. Gold circlets ringed his stretched earlobes. The color of his skin was deep reddish brown like Buck had never seen.

"You made it."

"You expected me?"

"For many days now."

"Where is this place?"

"It is the edge of the world."

In Buck's state of altered consciousness, the old man's answer didn't seem particularly odd.

"Why am I here?"

"For answers."

"I don't even know the questions."

"Few people do."

"I have never experienced a place such as this. It's almost like I'm in a dream."

"Maybe you are," the old man said.

"But I am fully aware of everything around me. If you cut me, I'm sure I would bleed. This is real."

"Even dreams are real."

"Then am I dreaming?"

The old man didn't answer his question. "You have passed every test so far. There are more."

"What tests?"

"You were wise not to follow the crow. You are also wise enough to believe in omens." He pointed to the feather still in Buck's hair. "Omens do not always signal something good or bad. Sometimes they simply indicate the path you should follow."

"What now?"

"You must drink from the black cup."

An earthen vat sat beside the fire and the old man produced a black cup made from what looked like a conch shell. Engraved symbols with meanings Buck didn't grasp decorated the cup and reminded him of Esme's tattoo. He dipped it into the vat, and then held it to his lips and drained it. When the last drop dribbled from the corners of his mouth, he plunged it again into the vat.

"Now you must drink," he said, handing Buck the ceremonial cup.

Dark brown, almost black liquid filled the vessel. Buck took it and put it to his lips, frowning from the bitter taste as he drained it. The old man nodded his approval. Dipping the cup into the vat again, he drank all of it for a second time, then filled it again and handed it to Buck.

Seeing his grimace, the old man smiled. "Are you okay?"

"This tastes awful, what is it?"

"Asi, the tea of truth."

Whatever was in the drink caused Buck's head to buzz and his body to shake. The reaction grew more intense after two more cups of the hot liquid.

"Asi removes all sin and purifies the soul. Drink more," he said, handing Buck yet another cup of the strong liquid.

The old man finally sat the black cup on the ground and lit a ceremonial pipe. After a long pull, he handed it to Buck, the first puff he took so strong it almost caused his eyes to cross. Grinning when he saw Buck's grimace, the old man led him outside. Beauty didn't follow them as they took a narrow pathway to the top of the sheer rock cliff behind the cabin. The old man stopped at the edge of the cliff where it overlooked the pristine lake. Bending forward, he closed his eyes and vomited over the precipice.

"If you are to find wisdom, you must purge yourself of whatever evil lives in your body."

Buck approached the precipice, bent forward and vomited the strong black beverage out of his system. As he wiped his mouth with the back of his hand, he realized the old man was still holding his other arm. He continued doing so, leading him back down the path and into the cabin.

Returning to his place beside the fire, the Old man relit the pipe and puffed it. "Now you are cleansed. Now you can see the truth."

"I see nothing. Please help me."

The old Indian handed Buck the cloud blower and waited until he puffed the strong tobacco.

"You are in danger. You have wandered into the realm of two evil spirits."

"The panther?"

"Yes, at least in one of his guises. The panther, or the spirit the big cat sometimes represents, is a shape-shifter. He has come to your world to avenge a wrong. You are not the target but you are still in danger."

"Beauty saved me from the cat. She is fearless."

"Beauty embodies perfect goodness; the single element evil can never overcome. She saved you once but cannot help you if she is not around."

"You spoke of two evils."

"Yes, one ancient evil spirit has taken the form of a man in your world, but he is not really a man."

The old Indian nodded when Buck asked, "The one called Jimmy Quick?"

"He senses you are after him and he will kill you if he can."

Buck stared at the old man through dilated eyes. "What is your name?"

"That is not important."

"Then at least tell me if this is a dream."

"No my son, this is very real."

***

Buck awoke in the teepee lying between Esme and Kristy, the old Indian's words still echoing in his head. He had many questions for Esme, but didn't get to ask them because she hurriedly left the teepee.

"Where is she going?"

Kristy stretched and yawned. "As our spiritual leader, she has her morning duties, like greeting the dawn on the eastern perimeter."

"I have some questions for her."

"Today is a holy day and she won't return until after dark."

"She is a strange and beautiful woman. Where is she from?"

"She is from here," Kristy said.

"You mean Logan County?"

"No, here, this spot. Esme has always been here."

Buck didn't know what to make of Kristy's double talk but decided to take it as an "I do not know."

She smiled and kissed him then got out of bed to get dressed. Buck stayed under the covers, watching her young and bountiful naked body. She didn't seem to mind.

"Will you return tonight?"

"Maybe," he said. "But I have a few things on my plate I need to clean off first."

Chapter 20

Buck went to Sunset Farms to feed Pard and the horses. It was already mid-afternoon when he discovered he'd left his cell phone in the Navigator. He had ten missed calls when he finally checked them. One was from Beth and it was the first call he returned.

"The doctors sent Trey home last night. He wants to see you."

"Great news. Is it okay if I come by?"

"I'd be upset if you didn't. Come have lunch with him at the Pendant."

Buck glanced at his old Rolex. "It's a little late for lunch."

Beth laughed. "No problem. I have an in with the cook."

"I'm on my way."

It was closer to dinner than lunch when he finally joined Trey at a booth in Beth's Azure Pendant restaurant. Buck hugged him before he had a chance to say anything.

"Stop it, Cowboy. I hurt bad enough as it is. You're going to break my ribs."

"I should break your neck for getting shot."

"Boys, boys, if you two are going to squabble, then take it to the streets."

"Uncle," Buck said, raising his arms. "I'm too hungry to fight and it wouldn't be much of a challenge whipping up on an incapacitated man."

"That's the only way you'll ever whip me," Trey said.

Buck sat in the booth as Beth shook her head and returned to the kitchen. The interior of the Azure Pendant resembled a cozy hacienda, complete with Mexican tile floor, beamed ceiling and open hearth in the center. Hanging ferns and large potted plants helped separate the tables and provide a feel of spacious dining. Trey was drinking iced tea.

"Tea, huh? You really aren't feeling good, are you?"

"Doc said no alcoholic beverages while I'm on drugs and the Enforcer is making sure of it," Trey said, nodding toward Beth as she returned with a cold mug of Tecate for Buck.

"Sorry, Pal, I'll enjoy this one for both of us. You look good but how do you feel?"

"Not too bad except for the new tattoo on my back."

"Beth said you have some information."

"New info but not necessarily good. We were able to trace the ownership of the cattle-holding facility, but only to a nondescript LLC which doesn't seem to have any principals. We're still trying to track the ownership, but whoever formed it knows how to work the system."

"It's not part of Dunlap's ranch?"

"That's what's strange. It appears connected to the ranch and the people who work there also work for Dunlap. Someone has gone to great lengths to keep the two entities separate, at least of record."

"Where are all the cows going?"

Trey sipped his tea before answering. "We don't have a clue, but I have agents watching the facility."

"Our visit didn't seem to spook them. Why do you think that is?" Buck asked.

"There's a rival cattle rustling group operating

mostly in Texas. I bet those cowpokes thought we were part of that gang trying to establish a toehold in central Oklahoma. It's the only explanation I have."

"There are too many coincidences here for Dunlap not to be involved."

"I agree. Maybe you should check out his office and have a look at his files."

"You want me to break into his office?"

"Why not, you're pretty good at slipping locks. If he is involved, he has to keep books on the operation somewhere and he spends most of his time at Crescent Oil."

They dined on sour cream enchiladas and Buck drank another Tecate before saying goodbye to Trey and Beth. Many of the City's workforce were already making their way to various watering holes around town. A crowd had begun gathering in the Azure Pendant's bar as Buck headed toward the Petro Place, hoping to hatch a plan to get a look inside Roy Dunlap's office.

Most of Crescent Oil had already shut down for the day and had headed for Nick's. The boisterous crew welcomed him when he joined them. Georgia was alone and well into her cups. He noticed when she glanced at him with a drunken grin.

"Hi, Baby. I've been missing you," she said when she saw him.

"Where's Roy?"

"At the horse races in Hot Springs. I think he has another girlfriend over there."

"He is crazy if he does because she can't be as pretty as you are."

"Pretty doesn't matter with you men. You'd stick your dick in a Twinkie if you thought it would make you feel good."

"You're abusing the wrong man," he said. "I've never done you wrong, have I?"

Georgia touched his cheek and smiled. "Not yet, at

least."

"I'm not that way," he said.

"You are really cute and it makes me want to do something dirty with you, like give you a blow job under the table."

The two Tecate's had given him a buzz, along with the Wild Turkey and water Ronnie brought him when he sat down. Georgia was practically in his lap, her body heat already elevating his own temperature. His plan to get into Dunlap's office came together when she blew in his ear.

"You are mad at Roy."

"I'd like to scratch his eyes out," she said.

"If you're serious, I have a better idea for getting even with him."

"I'm all ears," she said.

"Roy must be an idiot to leave a gorgeous woman like you alone. We need to make him pay. Let's do it on his desk and really give him something to think about."

Georgia grinned. "I like it."

Almost everyone in the Crescent Oil group noticed when Buck and Georgia left the bar, smiling and waving, as if they were in on some secret. He didn't mind because he was feeling her soft warmth as she groped him in the elevator on the way upstairs. He didn't intend to have sex with Georgia. He only needed her to get into Roy's office so he could access his computer. Still, it didn't stop him from feeling like a total prick for using her to accomplish his goal.

"I can't remember the code with your tongue in my mouth," she said as she punched in numbers at the front door.

Despite her admonition, the light on the keypad turned green and she entered with no alarm sounding. Buck held her hand as she led him down the hall to Dunlap's office.

"Roy is a stickler for security. He will die when he realizes we were in his office after hours."

Georgia chuckled as she punched in Roy's code. They were barely inside his office before she had strewn half her clothes across the expensive Oriental carpet. Buck wondered, as she began emulating a female possessed by a sexual demon, if he would accomplish anything other than unbridled sex with a scorned woman. She loosened his belt, unbuttoned his jeans and began groping his private parts, stopping abruptly when she sensed he wasn't cooperating.

"What's the matter?"

"This sounded like a good idea downstairs but now I just can't do it."

"You think I don't know why we're here? I want you as much as you want me."

"I'm having a conscience attack. This just isn't right."

"To hell with your conscience! All my friends downstairs saw us leave together and I'm sure every one of them thinks we're having sex right now. I'm going to give you a blowjob and you are going to like it. When we go back downstairs and everyone is looking at us, I want your tongue halfway down my throat and your hands on my ass. You got it, Cowboy?"

"Yes ma'am," Buck said as Georgia continued working on him.

Soon in the throes of passion, he moaned, unable to mask the pleasurable sensations coursing through his body. Georgia didn't stop until he had climaxed and a gratified gasp escaped his lips. When he unclenched his jaw and fists, he stared into her smiling eyes.

"Oh my God! I think I've died and gone to heaven."

"More?" she asked.

"I can't take anymore," he said, sitting up and rubbing his forehead, his senses slowly starting to return.

Georgia fished around in her purse until she found her cell phone. After returning Buck's exposed member into her mouth, she clicked away several pictures, and then directed them to her email address. When she finished with him, she cranked up Roy's computer and downloaded the picture to the desktop, leaving it as the background on his screen.

"You know his password? Buck asked, beginning to recover.

"I know everything about him, including his underwear size. His password is cowdaddy."

"Roy will fire you when he sees this."

"Cards laid are cards played," she said, her words a drunken slur.

Georgia was done, both literally and figuratively. Buck wrestled her clothes back on her as best he could and returned with her to the basement bar. She was feeling the effects of the alcohol she had consumed. When they joined the Crescent crew, she forgot about Buck's tongue, and his hands groping her ass.

"She's had it," he told Sandy. "Would you mind taking her home? I have some more work to do upstairs."

"Looks to me like you've already done some work upstairs," she said with a grin.

Despite their ribbing, Sandy and Ty agreed to drive Georgia home. Buck returned to the Crescent Oil offices. He'd watched Georgia use Roy's keypad and hoped intense sexual excitement hadn't caused him to forget the code. The door opened with no problem and he shut it behind him before proceeding to the computer.

The screen fired to life again when he entered the password, the lascivious picture greeting him as Roy's new screen background. Feeling a twinge of guilt, he changed the background and deleted the picture from the computer. No need tipping him off someone had accessed his private information.

Most of the files on Dunlap's computer concerned Crescent Oil business. He soon learned Roy kept two sets of oil well pumping and gauging reports, one showing actual production, the other altered production. Roy, it seems, was stealing his own company's oil. Try as he might, he could find no reference to a cattle operation, illegal or otherwise. Roy was more cautious than he had thought. Maybe he wasn't as cautious with his emails.

Buck clicked on Roy's desktop email basket, trying to access it using the password cowdaddy. Cowdaddy didn't work, nor cowdaddy1, but cowdaddy10 did. He checked Roy's emails. Since Dunlap's email server was not web-based, he knew he would have to glean what information he could before leaving the office.

The Petro Place had a night watchman and Buck had met the young man on more than one occasion. He didn't want to explain what he was doing in Roy's office, so he began work at once. Dunlap took care of his emails in a meticulous manner, all sorted alphabetically in folders. One folder labeled Molasse had more than a hundred entries, many referring to the sale of cattle. Buck had a tiny jump drive attached to his keychain he used to store information from his computer. Inserting it into a USB port, he copied the entire Molasse file, and the records implicating Dunlap in theft of Crescent Oil crude. He was busy visually scanning some of the other files when he heard someone outside the door.

He would have some explaining to do no matter who found him sitting at Roy's computer. Crawling under the desk, he pulled the office chair in front of him. The door opened but no one entered, and he held his breath until the person shut the door.

He listened to footsteps padding down the hallway, stopping periodically to randomly check an office door. Hoping the folders he had copied contained valuable information, he waited a moment to make sure no one was in the hall. When he opened the door, he got the surprise of his life.

Chapter 21

The person in the hallway was as surprised to see him, as he was to see her.

"Georgia, what in the hell are you doing here?"

"I got to thinking about the picture we left on Roy's computer screen and decided I needed to delete it."

Buck lowered his eyes and rubbed his forehead. "I beat you to the punch."

Still woozy from all the alcohol she had consumed, she didn't question his story. Instead, she said, "Good, because I would just die if Roy had found our picture."

"It's gone. I'll show you if you like."

"I trust you," she said, making him feel like an even bigger heel than he already did.

"Sandy said she would take you to your house."

"She did, but I caught a cab back because I was shaking when I woke up on the couch."

"It's all right now. I'll take you home."

Georgia huddled against the passenger-side door during the short ride, her arms tightly folded.

"You know what we did doesn't mean anything to me. I was only using you to get back at Roy. Can you forgive me?"

"You were drunk and I took advantage of you."

"You are full of yourself, Buck McDivit. I haven't

had sex with anyone I didn't want to since I was seventeen, no matter how drunk I was."

"That's good to know. I wouldn't want to come between you and Roy."

This time Georgia laughed. "I'm not ready to call it quits with him yet, but I am this close," she said, measuring an inch with her thumb and forefinger.

"When you decide to quit him, I know someone you might like."

"You are a real hunk but, no offense, I like older men."

"Not me, someone else."

"I'll keep it in mind."

Buck let the subject drop. "Have you ever heard of the Molasse Company?"

Georgia nodded. "I didn't tell you everything I know about Jimmy Quick."

"Oh?"

"He works for Molasse and Roy does business with them."

"What kind of business?"

"You know how secretive Roy is. When I asked him, he got defensive and told me it wasn't any of my business."

"What does Quick do for them?"

"He provides security, sort of like a bodyguard. It must be important because they pay him lots of money."

"Even more than he makes fighting dogs and chickens?" Georgia shook her head. "Did Roy know about Frankie Boggs?"

Georgia nodded. "Roy doesn't want to marry me but he doesn't want anyone else to either."

"You had an affair with Frankie?"

"We were close friends and had sex from time to time."

"And KK?"

"KK and I are best friends. She likes who I like, and

vice-versa. Neither of us are virgins, you know. Stop looking at me like I'm some sort of a whore."

"Sorry," he said, turning away. "I'm not exactly a saint myself."

"That's a fact," she said. "I've known Billy goats less horny than you."

She laughed aloud when he said, "Baa!"

Georgia wouldn't let him walk her to the door of her house. She stood outside the Navigator, standing on her tiptoes to kiss him goodnight through the window.

"Did you delete the picture of us off your cell phone," he asked.

"The caller's picture shows up on the screen when my phone rings. I can hardly wait until you call," she said with a wanton grin.

***

Buck suddenly had more information than he could digest. He had never known his real mother or father, Sheriff Hagen and his wife Carol, the closest he had ever come. Hagen had rescued him from juvenile detention, inviting him to spend the weekend at his little farm outside of Guthrie. It was Sheriff Hagen who taught him how to ride a horse, but it was his wife Carol who had instructed him how to be a better person. Buck needed motherly advice and Carol Hagen was the only person who could come close to filling the bill. He headed the Navigator north on I-35 toward the Hagen's farm.

The night was warm so he opened the sliding roof and stared up at the sky. Stars and moon were clearly visible but fast moving clouds, blowing in from the southwest, were beginning to cover them. He shut the moon roof when a light sprinkle of rain began to fall. Not bothering to turn on the radio, he let darkness and silence encompass him. After taking the Stillwater highway out of Guthrie, he turned north.

The Hagen's lived on a farm at the literal end of

the road. He found their front gate open, almost as if they were expecting him, and he pulled to a stop by their front porch. The couple was sitting in the darkness on the porch swing, enjoying the breeze whipped up by the approaching storm. Buck couldn't see, but he knew without looking they were holding hands.

"Carol said she thought you would come out tonight," Jim Hagen said.

"Smart woman. Way too smart for you, Sheriff."

Hagen grinned. "You're right. I don't know why she sticks around. Want a beer?"

"He doesn't need a beer," Carol said. "Get him a glass of ice tea."

"Yes dear," Hagen said, disappearing into the house.

Carol was a stunning fifty-something woman. She maintained her girlish figure by riding horses and working the park-like gardens surrounding their modern log cabin. Buck had always thought she was too pretty for Jim Hagen. Looks didn't always matter. Hagen possessed other important things like brains and integrity. Buck sat on the porch, dangling his boots over Carol's purple irises.

"What's the problem?" she finally asked.

"I got my best friend shot. I'm over thirty and never been married. Hell, I don't even have a steady girlfriend."

"When you're ready to settle down, and you aren't, you'll find the right woman," she said.

Lightning flashed across the sky, followed by a loud clap of thunder.

"I don't deserve the right woman. I'm a whore-dog and even my best friend can't trust me."

Buck grinned when she said, "Would it make you feel better if I told you no one is perfect?"

"You are."

Carol laughed. "Far from it. I probably aged my

poor mother, God rest her soul, by at least twenty years because of my wild ways."

"I'm talking about other things."

"We are talking about the same thing, Buck McDivit. You are feeling guilty because of Trey, but Jim said he is going to be just fine. You would have done the same for him."

"Maybe, but it's not the only thing bothering me."

"Tell me," she said.

"It's kind of embarrassing."

"I'm a grown woman. I can take it."

"I'm seeing two women at the same time. A three-way, if you get my drift."

Carol didn't immediately react and Buck knew if he could see her through the darkness, her mouth would be open.

"Oh shit!" she finally said. "You have to be kidding me."

"I knew you wouldn't like it," he said.

"Because it's unacceptable. How did you get into this situation?"

"Gonads originally. Now I'm not sure."

"Which means?"

"What I mean is I like the relationship. I like both women. I think I may even love both of them. It just seems natural."

"Maybe you better explain this relationship to me so I can relate." Buck proceeded to tell her about Lykaia, Esme and Kristy. When he finished, she said, "I don't like it one little bit but nothing you have told me so far should give you a guilty conscience, at least as long as you have no commitment to either woman, or they to you. There must be something else."

Reluctantly, Buck told her about spending the night with KK, and even his tryst with Georgia. She just shook her head.

"You are spinning your wheels with KK, have been for years. Georgia is another matter. I can't condone it.

You should be a better person."

Rain began falling again, this time more than a sprinkle. Buck pulled himself out of the irises, beneath the porch roof, and put his arms around Carol.

"I'm sorry," he said. "Can you forgive me?"

She hugged him. "You are a big boy, Buck McDivit. I can't live your life for you. You'll have to do it yourself."

"Did I miss something?" Jim Hagen asked when he returned.

"You know very well you did, you big lug," Carol said. "Buck and I had a nice conversation and now I am going to bed. I think you two might have a few things to discuss without me around."

Hagen handed Buck a beer as Carol kissed them both goodnight and departed the front porch.

"Screw the ice tea. I brought us each a Coors. Looks like another storm brewing."

"Now I know why you keep getting elected year after year," Buck said.

"No thanks to you. Why are you so down in the mouth?"

"Is it that apparent?"

"You look like a spanked puppy. Tough night?"

"It's my cattle rustling investigation. Every time I think I'm getting someplace, I step off into another hole."

Buck had returned to his perch on the side of the porch and Jim joined him.

"Trey is keeping me abreast."

"I'm working on some new information and this is lots bigger than a renegade cowboy stealing a few head of cattle."

The Hagen's farm lay so far in the woods, you could barely hear the semis passing on I-35. Buck remained silent for a moment, listening to night sounds and the patter of rain on the roof.

"I learned something tonight about the operation.

Roy Dunlap is doing business with a company called Molasse. Jimmy Quick works both for Roy and for the company as a bodyguard."

"What else?"

"Frankie Boggs, the man murdered on Clayton's farm, was playing around with Dunlap's girlfriend and he got wind of it."

"Satchel seems to think the murder was passion related. You think Dunlap had Frankie Boggs murdered?"

"Not only that, I think Jimmy Quick is the man who murdered him."

"Let me get us another beer." When Jim returned, thunder rumbled in the distance and the earthy odor of rain-soaked dust saturated the air. "Now finish your story."

"There is a large cattle operation just north of Crescent, not far from the trailer community. Trey and I are sure there is stolen cattle there. He checked into the ownership, but it seems untraceable for some reason. It doesn't really matter because it's connected to Dunlap's ranch and the hands apparently work at both places."

Lightning suddenly flashed across the sky followed by a nearby clap of thunder. Wind had also picked up, blowing in gusts from the west. Jim gazed up at the sky.

"We have no evidence Quick had anything to do with Boggs' murder."

"Hard to believe. Are you sure?"

"Satchel wasn't able to turn up a lick of evidence, not even a single clue."

"How is it possible?"

Hagen shook his head. "I'll look into Molasse for you tomorrow. Have you told anyone else?"

"You're the first to hear about it, Boss."

"I'm not your boss. If I were, I'd fire you. What about the man stalking the compound?"

"Everything has come up a blank."

"You haven't learned anything?"

"Not what I said."

"What then?"

"Do you believe in the supernatural?"

Jim didn't have time to answer. With an old flannel robe she wore both winter and summer wrapped tightly around her pajamas, Carol appeared on the porch, a lantern flailing in one hand, Goldie, her orange tabby squirming under her arm.

"There's a tornado on the ground heading our way."

"Where's Snuffy? Jim asked, suddenly excited.

"His bed in the kitchen. I couldn't wake him."

Buck hurried to the barn, shooing the horses and other animals into open pasture. Jim ran into the house to retrieve his dog. It was raining hard when they reached the storm shelter. Buck pulled open the heavy door and hurried inside. Wind had increased exponentially in a short time and was already blowing in ninety-mile-per-hour straight-line gusts when he latched the heavy storm shelter door.

"I hate these things," Carol said, sitting on a bench and nervously stroking the cat as she listened to the storm raging outside the shelter between warnings on the weather radio.

Jim had a flashlight and did a quick search for spiders and snakes. Finding none, he sat beside Carol and put his arm around her. Snuffy never missed a beat, curling up beneath their feet and closing his eyes. For the next twenty minutes, they listened as heavy rain, wind and hail pounded the shelter, and watched fitfully as the heavy storm door heaved like a distance runner's lungs, trying repeatedly to fly away into the dark Oklahoma night.

"Night time tornadoes are the worst," Jim said, stating a fact all three long-time residents of central Oklahoma already knew.

Rainwater dripped through cracks in the roof,

dampening the shelter seekers, Carol's tabby and sleeping Snuffy. Finally, the outside cacophony subsided.

The storm had passed, heading east. Buck unlatched the heavy storm door and pushed it open. What greeted them looked like a bizarre scene from a Kafka tale.

Chapter 22

Dime-sized hail covered the ground, looking like the aftermath of a winter ice storm. Light from the moon behind the clouds reflected off the hail, creating an eerie glow. An oak tree lay felled not ten feet from the shelter, its large trunk shattered and uprooted.

Jim dodged his way through debris strewing the ground as he sprinted toward the house. Buck and Carol found him staring at the roof. As they assessed the damage, the clouds opened to a heavy downpour of warm spring rain. Carol didn't wait, running inside to see what, if anything remained. The roof had a fair-sized hole, mostly over the bedroom, many of the windows blown out.

Buck shouted. "You got a tarp or something to cover the hole?"

"In the barn, if we still have one."

Buck sprinted toward it, Jim right behind him. Destructive tornadoes often cut very narrow swaths, leaving some buildings destroyed while the house next door may have no damage at all. They found the barn untouched. Jim quieted the three horses straggling back from the pasture and then climbed into the loft to retrieve a large tarp.

"There's a ladder against the wall, and rope and

bungee cords in the bin over there.”

The downpour continued as Buck and Jim climbed up on the roof and situated the tarp over the gapping opening. Water raced down their necks but the high winds had thankfully moved east. Carol met them with towels as they raced into the kitchen.

“There are dry clothes in the bathroom.”

***

They sat at the kitchen table drinking strong coffee when Jim began to laugh. His amusement was contagious and they all laughed. When Carol’s laughter finally ceased, she started to cry.

“It’s all right, Baby. No one got hurt and the horses and other animals are fine. I’ll start cleaning this mess up tomorrow.”

“I’ll help,” Buck said.

“No you won’t. You may have damage at your own place you have to clean up.”

“Let’s hope not,” Carol said. “It’s after midnight so you are staying here tonight. We’ll get a good night’s sleep and I’ll fix us all a country breakfast in the morning. Then we can assess the damage.”

“I’m worn out so you don’t have to twist my arm,” Buck said.

He had spent many nights in Jim and Carol’s spare bedroom. This particular night, he was asleep almost as soon as his head hit the pillow.

***

Buck awoke to the sound of light rain on the windowpane and aroma of bacon and eggs coming from the kitchen. He found Carol and Jim sitting at the table, drinking coffee.

“Good thing we got the tarp up,” Jim said. “It rained all night.”

“Do you have much damage inside the house?”

“Nothing we can’t dry out. Everything survived except for part of the roof. I have an insurance adjuster on his way to take a look.”

"And all the animals are okay," Carol added. "What a blessing."

Buck offered again to help clear the rubble. Jim and Carol both told him to go home and check his own place.

***

Buck headed south on Highway 74 when he noticed a fast approaching vehicle in his rearview mirror. He was doing seventy and guessed the vehicle's speed at ninety, or better. When it neared his rear bumper without trying to pass, he crowded the shoulder of the road. They were on a long stretch of straight highway with nothing coming in the opposite direction. The driver of the bright blue pickup behind him didn't attempt to pass him, slowing just enough to tuck in less than a few feet away.

Buck took his foot off the gas. When he did, he got a surprise. The truck banged into him hard enough to propel him into the ditch. Fighting the steering wheel, he straightened the path of the Navigator, but only for a moment. The pickup followed him off the road and struck him again.

With barely a moment to glance in his mirror, he saw the blue pickup had a cattle-catcher type bumper extending above its hood. Like a deranged NASCAR driver, the person in the truck began using the bumper to pound the rear of the Navigator. Buck somehow made it back up on the blacktop without crashing.

Realizing now the person in the pickup was deliberately trying to wreck him, he attempted a more radical evasive maneuver, swerving hard left, and then right, hoping to shake the vehicle pasted to his rear end. The person in the truck behind him was obviously an expert driver because nothing he did managed to shake him off his bumper.

The truck banged against him for what seemed an interminable time, but was in actuality less than a minute before finally running him into the ditch again.

The Navigator banged into the deep trench, Buck trying to steer his way out of it until the airbag deployed. When he opened his eyes, he was in the Navigator, the vehicle lying on its side.

Buck struggled to loosen the seat belt, finally succeeding. He climbed out the smashed window with great difficulty, someone grabbing his arms to help him. In his stupor, he hoped it wasn't the driver of the blue pickup. It wasn't. Four roughnecks, on their way home following their shift on a drilling rig, had eased him out of the truck and laid him in the grass.

"You all right?" one of them asked. "We saw the truck that ran you off the road."

Holding his head, Buck asked, "Did you get his tag number?"

"Couldn't miss it," one of the men with oily faces said. "It was a big Q."

Buck didn't reply, blacking out from the impact of the crash.

***

Next time he opened his eyes, Clayton O'Meara was staring back at him.

"You okay?" he asked.

Buck grabbed the top of his head and winced. "I think I'm going to throw up."

A nurse whose nametag said Estelle put a pan under his chin and held it there as he vomited uncontrollably.

"Sorry," he said as the nurse got rid of the pan and wiped his face with a damp towel.

"Don't worry about it Sweetie," she said. "It's my job."

"What happened?" he asked Clayton, still standing there with a beleaguered expression on his face.

"You tell me. State troopers called to say my vehicle was in the ditch, the driver taken to the Guthrie Hospital emergency room."

"Sorry about the truck."

"I have plenty of insurance. We're you drunk?"

Buck didn't have to answer because someone walked up behind them and spoke for him.

"Alcohol had no part in the accident. Mr. McDivit's blood-alcohol content was normal. I'm Doctor Lee and I'll be looking after you."

The tall doctor with the gentle voice opened one of Buck's eyelids and stared into his eye as he shined a light into it. Satisfied by what he saw, he patted Buck's shoulder and returned the damp washcloth to his eyes. Clayton was not ready to let the matter drop.

"If he wasn't drunk, why the hell did he run off the road at ten in the morning?"

"A truck forced me into the ditch," Buck said, memory of the event slowly returning.

"You have a severe concussion but nothing is broken," the soft-spoken Doctor Lee said. "I'm admitting you for observation. You need to stay here for twenty-four hours."

"You tried to put your head through the roof when you hit the ditch," Clayton said. "Why would someone run you off the road?"

Talking was making him nauseous again and Estelle appeared with the pan and towel. The doctor intervened with Clayton.

"We'll put him on a drip and administer acetaminophen." Turning to Buck, he said, "I know you don't feel very good right now but you'll be fine in a day or so."

After patting Buck's shoulder, he hurried away to treat another patient. Estelle gave him a dose of something for the nausea, for which he was grateful. Clayton took care of all the details, and then rejoined him in his room.

"Now tell me again what happened."

Buck grimaced and grabbed his head. "I was on my way home when someone in a blue pickup started banging my rear bumper. It wasn't an accident. He was intentionally trying to run me off the road. After he ran me into the ditch, some roughnecks stopped and pulled me out of the truck."

"Why would someone try to kill you?" Clayton asked.

Buck cleared his throat. The fluids and pain medicine had started working and he felt almost well enough to answer.

"Have you ever heard of a company named Molasse?"

Clayton shook his head. "Sounds familiar for some reason but I can't place it."

The rancher waited for more answers when a floor nurse insisted that he leave. Buck's head felt better when she closed the blinds and turned off his lights. He soon dozed off into a fitful sleep.

Chapter 23

Buck got little rest that night with nurses checking on him every thirty minutes. Whenever he dozed off, they would wake him and stare into his eyes with a small flashlight. Toward dark, he was feeling hungry and one of the nurses brought him some peach yogurt. His nausea had slowly abated until he was finally able to eat a little food without immediately throwing it up. He didn't know until then he even liked peaches.

Pumped full of fluids, he took many shaky trips to the bathroom, rolling his IV along the floor and not worrying about his bare butt protruding from the back of the hospital gown. At one point, he felt strong enough to look into the closet and found his clothes and cell phone. His keychain was intact but the attached jump drive missing. When he inspected his aching left shoulder, he saw someone had incised the letter Q into it. It made him realize the big dog fighter's knife had been close enough to his throat to cut it, if he had wanted to.

No missed calls. Clayton must have gotten the word out. This made him wonder why no one had stopped by to see him. The night nurse solved the mystery.

"Doctor Lee is restricting visitors. What you need

is undisturbed rest."

Buck agreed but wondered why it didn't include the nurses, waking him every time he closed his eyes. When the last nurse left the room, he dialed Lana.

"Are you okay?"

"I can't recall having a headache like the one I have now. Kristy said you have connections in the business world. I was wondering if you could check on a company for me."

Buck explained to Lana about Molasse Limited, and then put the cell phone under his pillow so the nurses wouldn't take it away from him. He needn't have bothered as he got no calls that night, nor did he make any more. He finally got a few hours of sleep between visiting nurses and trips to the bathroom. The next time he awoke, it was morning and he was staring up into the face of the man with the same pleasant voice as the doctor who had admitted him.

"How do you feel?"

Doctor Lee laughed when Buck answered, "Like warmed over shit."

Doctor Lee was fifty-something, and had striking eyes which must have made all the nurses swoon when he was younger. Buck liked him instantly and realized it was because of his friendly smile and gentle voice.

"I feel lots better. When can I go home?"

"You sustained a nasty concussion but you are much better now. I'm releasing you and there is someone here to pick you up."

The door opened and Kristy, radiant in a tailored business dress, hugged him. Doctor Lee gave Buck several prescriptions and said farewell. Kristy wheeled him to the elevator, and outside to her Prius.

"Nice ride," he said as she handed him a pair of dark sunglasses.

"They said you might be sensitive to sunlight."

Buck didn't realize how sleepy he was. Soon as he laid his head back against the rest, he fell asleep and didn't awaken until Kristy stopped the hybrid in one of Lykaia's underground parking lots.

"Stay put," she said, opening the door and coming around the car to help him. "You are probably still a little shaky."

"More than just a little," he said, light-headed as he climbed from the car.

Kristy made a call on her cell phone, a woman in an electric vehicle soon joining them. She took them to Esme's teepee and dropped them off. Esme was outside, waiting for them. Although he didn't feel helpless, he reveled in the attention they paid him, helping him into the teepee. After laying him on soft bedding, Esme and Kristy began removing his clothing.

"I'm not an invalid, you know?"

"Stop bellyaching," Esme said.

Kristy tucked him beneath the covers and Esme dabbed his face with an aromatic potion.

"This is soothing and it has an herbal ingredient which will prevent you from loosing consciousness."

"I'll bet it won't keep me from falling asleep. The nurses at the hospital kept me awake all night and I can't recall ever being this tired."

"You can sleep now without worry. You will awaken fully refreshed."

Buck dozed off shortly after closing his eyes, awakening some twelve hours later, Beauty's tongue licking a warm swath across his face.

"Hey girl," he said, hugging her. "Did you miss me?"

Beauty had apparently missed him, or else was putting on a good act. She even almost wagged her tail. Kristy had already left for work, but Esme joined them and rubbed balm on his bruises.

"How do you feel this morning?"

"I don't know what sort of potion you put on my face, but you should patent it. I slept like a baby."

Esme had a bowl of something she spoon-fed to

him. It tasted like cornmeal and chicken broth and he felt better after eating it. She also gave him herbal tea which reminded him of the concoction he drank from the old Indian's black cup.

Esme smiled when he finished. "The sleep, poultices and nourishment will help return your strength. Now, there are things we must discuss."

"Sounds ominous."

"More than you know," she said.

"Then don't keep me in suspense."

"Not here, at a place not far away. Can you walk?"

Buck nodded. "I'm a little shaky on my feet but I think what's causing it is the tea you gave me."

He felt woozy as he pulled the covers away, glancing around for something to wear.

"No need for clothes where we are going."

She took his hand and led him along a path through the forest until they arrived at what seemed to him the very same clearing where he had met the old Indian. The old man's cabin was gone, but not the tranquil sound of falling water. A small waterfall plunged from the cliff, the pool beneath it so clear and blue he could see every detail of its sandy bottom. Esme stripped away her clothes and led him into the pool.

"Where are we?"

"We have crossed," she said.

The clearing seemed exactly as he remembered it, except with no ground fog or giant butterflies. Esme swam toward the eddy beneath the falling water and he followed her. Swimming beneath the waterfall, she stopped just inside the mouth of a small grotto and sat on the sandy bottom.

"Where is the old Indian?" he asked.

"Everywhere; he is with us now."

"How is it possible?"

She didn't answer his question. "Close your eyes and count to ten before you open them."

She was gone when he opened his eyes. "Where are you?"

"Beside you," she said, giving him a start.

When he turned, she was sitting on the other side of him.

"Great trick. How did you do it?"

Her image glimmered, and then disappeared as he looked at her. She appeared again in her original position.

"You think I'm tricking you? Maybe I have you drugged and hypnotized. You wouldn't know if I did."

"No, I wouldn't. Am I?"

"No more than normal," she said, smiling. "We are sitting in the Pool of Life. Look at your bruises."

Buck glanced at his arms and legs, his bruises gone, the letter Q Jimmy Quick cut into his shoulder now nonexistent."

"This must be a dream," he said.

"Can't you tell the difference between a dream and reality?"

He didn't have an answer. One thing seemed very real to him—the warmth and proximity of her body. He had never seen her in the full light of day before. Her dark hair was close to black, her eye color also black, but with a luminous purple tinge. Every feminine turn of her body was perfect and her face caused him to think of a beautiful Mayan maiden, complete with ceremonial tattoo. She smiled when she noticed him staring at her.

"Like what you see?"

"You already know the answer. Why did you bring me here?"

"You are being tested. That is why I had you withhold information about the panther attack. You are also in grave danger and as much as I love you, it is beyond my power to protect you."

"Jimmy Quick?"

"He means to kill you and drag you to hell.

Another spirit has followed him from the Underworld. It is the shape-shifter, Quick's bitter enemy. He'll take you too, if he can."

***

It was dark when Buck awoke again. This time he felt strong when he stood. The fire in the center of the teepee emitted only faint illumination, but he could see his bruises were gone. He pulled a colorful serape over his shoulders and joined Esme, Beauty and Kristy outside as they watched a pot simmer over an open fire.

"We thought you were going to sleep all day and through the night," Kristy said. "How do you feel?"

"Wonderful, except for the strange dreams the blow to my head seems to have caused."

Esme smiled and Beauty strode over to him, demanding a few caresses, which he gladly bestowed. They shared the contents of the cooking pot with him—a well-seasoned stew which tasted wonderful, reminding him how hungry he was. Coyotes howled in the distance, their chorus accompanied by a nearby owl and an orchestra of crickets and tree frogs. Fireflies lighted the darkness of the surrounding forest, their ephemeral presence reminding him of a certain spirituality he couldn't quite remember.

"Lana will join us soon," Kristy said. "She has some information for you and wants to tell you in person."

Lana and Sara soon arrived at Esme's teepee.

"I can't believe you are up and around. Doctor Lee said the wreck could have killed you."

"You spoke with the doctor?"

"He is a friend of mine, a close friend."

The storms had dissipated, at least for the moment, the sky luminous with glowing stars and a golden moon which was almost full.

"Sara and I came for a soak in Esme's hot tub. If you join us, I will tell you what I found out about Molasse Limited."

Buck glanced at Esme for approval, but knew he needed none. She, along with Kristy, Sara and Lana, had already headed for the big wooden tub where they all began stripping off their clothes. He had almost gotten used to being nude in the midst of gorgeous naked women. It didn't stop him from blushing when Lana eyed him up one end and down the other. Darkness, thankfully, masked his flushed skin as he eased into the hot water.

"Lee said you left the hospital covered in bruises."

He smiled at Esme and said, "I know a wonderful medicine woman. Please tell me what you know about Molasse Limited."

"The company owns a fleet of specialized planes they use to transport horses to races around the world. British billionaires and Saudi sheiks are just part of their clientele. The business has evolved far beyond transporting race horses."

"How so?"

"Say a Kuwaiti businessman would like a Texas longhorn for his desert retreat. He can get one by contacting Molasse. If a rich Hong Kong merchant desires an African Snow Leopard, it can be had, also for a price."

"Molasse is dealing in stolen cattle and exotic animals?"

Lana nodded. "Some cattle breeds are guarded like a national treasure. Ranchers in New Zealand pay fortunes for exotic breeds rustled from Texas and Oklahoma."

"How did you learn about this?"

"An operation this big is hard to keep secret. I just asked the right people."

"Lana, you are wonderful."

Esme, Buck and Kristy laughed when Sara grabbed Lana's elbow and said, "Yes she is, and you need to keep your hands off her if you want to continue as the father of our child."

Morning Mist of Blood

Buck blinked. "What are you talking about?"
"I thought you knew. Lana is pregnant and you are the birth father."

Chapter 24

Buck lay beneath the covers in Esme's teepee, Kristy and Esme on either side of him.

Kristy touched his shoulder. "Why are you sulking? You're making me sad."

"I'm not the type of person who goes around spreading his seed. I always thought marriage was about spending your life with someone."

"What if Kristy and I were pregnant?"

"You aren't, are you?"

"No, but I don't recall you asking either of us if we are on birth control."

Buck grabbed his head and moaned. "I've spent my entire adulthood avoiding relationships because I didn't want a commitment. Now you tell me I have fathered a child by a woman I don't even remember sleeping with?"

Esme laughed. "You weren't exactly sleeping, not to mention you were the Fertility Deity during the spring equinox, the Prince of Spring and the best we've ever had. Just be thankful there is only one pregnant woman. Half the women in the compound might be with child by now, if there weren't certain rules."

"You have to be kidding me! Then the investigation was just a ruse to get me to the celebration."

"Lana is ruthless when it comes to achieving her goals," Kristy said.

"And her goal was to use me to father her child. Well I'm not going to let her get away with it."

"Lana won't let you have the child. She will raise him here at Lykaia and he will have the best upbringing and finest education possible. He will never want for anything."

"Not true. I've never known my real dad and I have regretted it every day of my life."

Kristy touched his cheek. "You are a special man. You deserved knowing the joy of a father and a mother. It won't be the case with your child. He'll have you for the rest of his life, and more mothers than he can handle."

The remainder of the night, Buck lay awake in the darkness between Esme and Kristy, pondering the situation. Esme snuggled against his shoulders and put her arm around him, massaging his chest. She kissed his neck and then whispered in his ear.

"I know you have doubts about becoming a father, but you had no choice in the matter. It was preordained."

***

Buck needed some answers. One of his questions was how could a forensic investigator as good as Satchel Pratt not have found a single scrap of evidence while investigating the murder of Frankie Boggs. He and Pard headed for Pratt's farm north of Guthrie to ask him. They found him sitting alone on his front porch swing.

"Damn, Brother, are you okay? Something must be up for you to drive all the way out here to see ol' Satchel."

Satchel was relaxing with a glass of vodka, water and ice. He could have been on his tenth one. You couldn't tell because he never acted drunk.

"Remember Pard? You were the one who named him."

Satchel smiled, grabbed his heart and said, "Hurt me, Brother. Need a beer?"

"You read my mind. I know where they are. Want another toddy?"

"You're the mind reader," Satchel said. "Vodka's on the kitchen cabinet. Now don't make me a pussy drink."

Satchel was rubbing Pard's ears when Buck returned with the vodka and beer and joined him on the swing.

"Nice night."

"You didn't come all the way out here to talk about the weather. What's up?"

"The Sheriff told me you didn't find a single usable clue in the Frankie Boggs murder."

"Nope, not one."

"How is it possible?"

"I've asked myself the same question a dozen times. It's not possible, or is it?"

Buck told him about Esme's two spirits from hell. "Do you believe in the supernatural?"

Satchel looked at him as if he were crazy. "Why hell no and neither do you. Sounds to me like you were fucked up on some hallucinogenic drug."

"But it would explain the lack of clues."

"Hell, Brother, you might as well say a magician made the clues disappear. Makes about as much sense and you know damn well it isn't the way things shake out."

Maybe he had been on hallucinogenic drugs, but after his visit with the old Indian and his dip in the magic pool with Esme, Buck wasn't sure what he believed anymore. He had wracked his brain for other possible explanations and had found none.

"I know the murderer killed Boggs with a knife and carved him up, but did you find any other non-lethal knife wounds on the body?"

"Like what?"

Satchel smiled when Buck said, "Like the letter Q?"

"Whoever killed Boggs carved the letter Q into his back. How did you know?"

"Trey had a Q carved in his back after the incident at the Rock Bar. Someone cut the same letter on my shoulder after running me off the road and almost killing me. I'm convinced the person responsible for all three acts is Jimmy Quick."

"Let me see the mark on your shoulder."

"It's gone."

"What do you mean it's gone?"

Buck grinned. "I know you don't believe in the supernatural, but Esme washed it away for me in the Pool of Life."

"I know it can't be the beer that's fried your brain. Exactly what are you smoking?"

He didn't wait for an answer, heading for the kitchen and returning shortly with vodka for himself and another Coors for Buck. "I didn't think I'd had that much to drink but I'm either hammered or else you are full of shit."

"Neither one, I hope," Buck said. "Jimmy Quick isn't my biggest problem now, anyway."

"Then maybe you better tell me what it is because ol' Satchel here is getting kind of confused."

"Welcome to the club. There was a woman I was going to fix you up with, but now I think she may be in on the con."

Buck told him the story of breaking into Roy Dunlap's office, omitting the part about the blow job.

"Georgia was the only person who knew I was in Dunlap's office. Someone tipped off Jimmy Quick. How else would he have known to take the jump drive off my keychain?"

"If you didn't tell her you had taken the

information on the jump drive, there's no way she could have known. You said Dunlap is a security freak. If so, he probably has an infrared spy camera in his office. You are lucky the cops didn't bust down the door and cart you off to jail."

Satchel's words made sense.

Buck shook his head. "Trey and I checked out a little community north of Crescent populated by bikers, meth cookers and general throwbacks."

"Hell, Brother, you wouldn't find a single honest person if you busted the whole place. That's why I keep an automatic weapon under the bed."

"Yeah, well we found something even more interesting when we drove past it—a holding pen big enough for a hundred head of cattle. We bluffed the guard and Trey got two blood samples. It's a good bet the two cows were stolen, but the evidence was illegally obtained and inadmissible."

"Did you check out the ownership of the holding pen?"

"An Australian company named Molasse Limited. Roy Dunlap is involved up to his neck. Only problem is, we have no real proof."

"You are pretty sure you know where they are taking the stolen cattle. Just get the place busted. You'll find the answers."

"How do I accomplish it without any evidence to get a warrant?"

"Why hell Brother, do what all good criminal detectives do when they reach a dead end. Pick your best suspect, concoct a story the authorities can buy into, tell it with a straight face and stick to it."

"What happens if we raid the place and find out it's a legitimate operation?"

"Hell, Brother, you're young and Mexico's not so far away. You might even find yourself a pretty senorita you really like down there."

Chapter 25

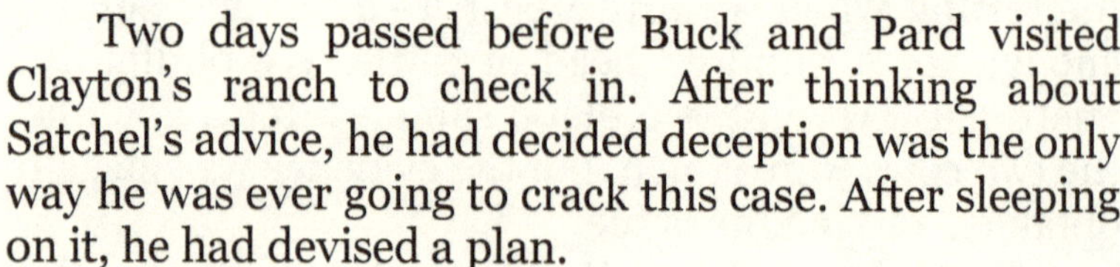

Two days passed before Buck and Pard visited Clayton's ranch to check in. After thinking about Satchel's advice, he had decided deception was the only way he was ever going to crack this case. After sleeping on it, he had devised a plan.

Satchel's words about Mexico kept echoing in his head as he patted Pard and told him to wait outside the house. If he were wrong about the cattle holding facility, he would have hell to pay. He thought about it as he climbed the steps to Clayton's veranda.

"Now where in the hell have you been?" Clayton asked, obviously upset he hadn't talked with the young man since he left the hospital.

"I wasn't feeling well so I just sort of crashed out for a few days. I'm ready to get back to work now."

"Glad to hear it. You totaled the Navigator so a new one's waiting for you in the parking lot."

"You didn't have to do that."

"I don't have to do anything. Now wait here while I go find Maria."

When Clayton disappeared down the hall, KK appeared from behind their bedroom curtain wearing little more than a sheer pink wisp of a baby doll nightgown. In tears, she hurried across the veranda and hugged him.

"Why didn't you call?" Buck had no good answer for her and cringed when she said, "I have something to tell you."

"Not something to do with our last night together, I hope."

KK's tears continued flowing freely. "Yes it does."

"Are you pregnant?"

"Why would you think that?"

"A wild guess," he said.

"That's not it. I know how much you love me. I love you too, but we have no future together. Clayton is my man now and I want you to forget me, at least as a lover, not as a friend."

"I'm happy for you and Clayton," he said as ingenuously as he could muster.

KK was smiling and hugging him when Clayton returned to the veranda. He frowned but didn't tell her to go put some clothes on, likely having already learned his lesson in that respect. It didn't matter because after a very intimate kiss with Buck, she hurried behind the curtain, back into the bedroom. She didn't return.

"I called the Sheriff and he's on his way over here. We have some talking to do."

Clayton relaxed in his serape-draped rocking chair and waited until Maria came with his whiskey and a stern look for Buck, along with a cup of black coffee. Sheriff Hagen arrived before he half finished it.

He demanded," Where in the hell have you been?"

"I was sort of whacked when I left the hospital. I've been pretty much out of it for the last few days."

"Carol and I were worried sick," he said.

"I know. I'm sorry."

"I've already given Buck a ration of shit," Clayton said. "Now we got other things to talk about."

"Tell me about the wreck." Hagen said.

Buck told him how someone in a blue pickup had deliberately run him off the road.

"I never saw the driver's face, but for my money it was Jimmy Quick."

"Buck seems to think he has valuable information."

"I'm listening."

"I told you about the cattle operation north of Crescent. Trey and I both believe it's where the rustlers are taking stolen cows. Well now I have proof."

Buck handed a sheet of paper to the Sheriff as Clayton craned to have a look.

"What is it?"

"A document linking Roy Dunlap to cattle rustling, and oil theft from Crescent Oil."

Sheriff Hagen frowned after scanning the instrument Buck had handed him. "This is pretty damning evidence. How did you obtain it?"

"I found it on Roy's computer at Crescent Oil."

"And what were you doing on Roy's computer?"

"Just looking."

"Then we can't use this. It's tainted."

"Bullshit!" Clayton said. "You're telling me we know who is stealing my cows, and my oil, and we can't do anything about it?"

"No judge would issue a warrant on the basis of this document, at least considering the way it was obtained."

"To hell, you say! I play poker or golf with practically every judge around. I'll get one to sign it tonight if we want."

"You sure about this, Buck? It would be my ass if we bust this place in error."

"Sheriff, I'm positive this cattle facility is involved in the cattle theft rampant around here."

"Well it's settled then," Clayton said, punching in a number on his cell phone. "I'm calling Judge Mannock right now. You get a warrant ready and I'll get it signed."

"I think we are moving a little too fast," Sheriff

Hagen said.

"The Lykaia compound has contacts all over the world and their head person, Lana, checked on Molasse Limited for me."

Buck told Hagen about the company and explained how it had evolved from primarily racehorse transportation to supplying rich people around the world, from Emirs to corporate CEO's, anything they might desire, even if it were stolen property.

Clayton said, "I know I'm not law enforcement, but however this thing shakes out, I want to be involved."

Chapter 26

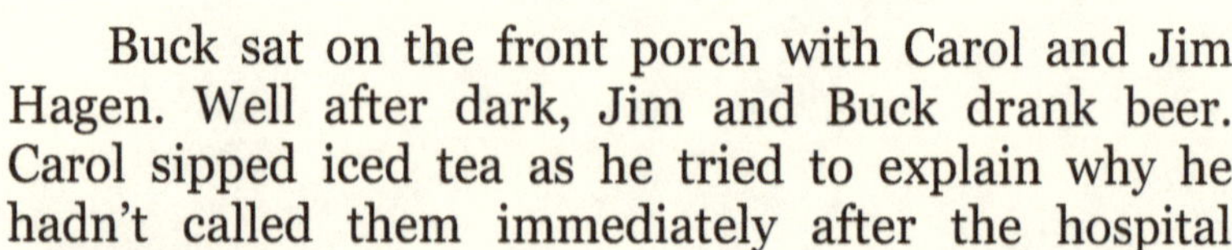

Buck sat on the front porch with Carol and Jim Hagen. Well after dark, Jim and Buck drank beer. Carol sipped iced tea as he tried to explain why he hadn't called them immediately after the hospital released him.

"I'm sorry. I had business I needed to attend to first."

Carol wasn't buying it. "I have known you since you were a snotty-nosed teenager. What was so important you couldn't have called and told me you were okay?"

"It's sort of complicated."

"No it isn't, you just don't want to tell me."

"Because I don't think its something you want to hear."

"Don't you trust me enough to tell me anyway?"

Jim Hagen was staying out of the argument, pacing the porch as he drank beer. Still, he missed none of the conversation.

Buck said, "You know I trust you."

"Now you are making me mad. You tell me now, Buck McDivit, and don't leave anything out."

Jim Hagen winced when Buck said, "I told you I am having sex with two women. Well, neither of them is pregnant." Carol started to say something, but Buck held up a hand. "They aren't, but another woman I didn't know I had sex with is."

Buck's admission was more than Jim Hagen could stand. "Now wait just a minute! You mean you got a woman pregnant you don't even remember sleeping with?"

"Drugs were involved."

"Oh? What kind of drugs and since when did you start using drugs?"

"I don't use drugs. They were Indian medicine drugs I took unwittingly during an ancient religious ceremony."

It was Carol's turn for her eyes to grow large. "An ancient religious ceremony?"

"Maybe more like a pagan revel."

Jim growled, "Have you flipped totally out?

"No, I haven't flipped out. Something just compromised my defenses."

"Like what?"

"A hundred or so gorgeous naked women."

Having no basis to comment, Jim and Carol simply stared at him in stunned disbelief.

"This is getting stranger by the minute," Carol finally said. "Maybe you better explain."

Buck told them about the spring solstice ceremony, leaving nothing out, except the parts he couldn't remember.

"Their religious tradition dictated I have sex with the secular head of Lykaia. I stayed over the next night because I thought I was working on an investigation. Whatever they put in my drink caused me to become sexually potent, so I'm glad their tradition stopped at one."

Following a derisive laugh, Jim asked, "So none of this is your fault?"

"Hell, how can you father a child and not be at fault? I'm not proud of what I did, but I take full responsibility."

Carol grabbed his hand. "Do the grandparents have any privileges?"

Buck smiled. "They may be pagans, but they aren't barbarians."

Having told Carol and Jim, the closest thing to parents he ever had, about his impending child lifted a huge weight from his shoulders. He wasn't prepared for Carol's reaction when Jim dropped yet another bomb on her.

"Buck and I have something else to tell you."

"As important as what I just heard?"

Jim nodded. "Different but just as important."

"Then I think you should wait a minute before you tell me," she said, leaving them and going into the house. She returned with a bottle of Weller's and three tumblers filled with ice. "Bottoms up," she said after pouring each of them a liberal portion of whiskey. "Now tell me what's so important."

Jim explained as briefly as possible about the illegal cattle operation. "We are going to bust the perps. Buck has asked to be involved and I have given my approval."

"Involved? What exactly do you mean?"

"I'm going to be part of the SWAT team."

"I see," she said. "First you tell me I'm about to have the grandchild I have prayed for all my life, and now you say their father may not be around to enjoy the baby with me?"

Buck just shook his head. "It's not so dangerous,"

"Jim, how dangerous is this operation?"

"Maybe you better give me more Weller's," he said.

Carol poured them all a fresh shot and then said, "Well?"

"It could be a little dangerous, but we'll have the advantage of surprise. We should have everything under control before a shot is fired."

Carol's mouth opened wide. "How many men are

involved?"

"I don't know, a hundred maybe."

"Good God, Jim! A hundred men?"

"There's lots of ground to cover."

She stared at Buck and said, "Not dangerous?"

"I was on the SWAT team when I was a cop in Oklahoma City. I took part in a couple dozen assaults and I never got hurt."

Carol started to cry." You got shot in the stomach once."

"Barely. A ricochet caught the bottom of my bulletproof vest. The bullet hardly penetrated the skin."

Carol slugged her shot of Weller's, poured herself another and drained it. Hurrying to the front door, she turned before entering. Tears streamed from her eyes as she pointed at Buck.

"Don't you dare get yourself killed and prevent me from seeing the only grandchild I'll probably ever have."

Buck and Jim watched her disappear into the house. Not bothering to pour himself a fresh shot of whiskey, he drank straight from the bottle and then handed it to Buck.

Buck followed suit with his own healthy swig and then said, "You okay?"

"I'm fine. It's just we've been married close to thirty years. I've been in mortal danger because of my job more times than I can count and Carol has never once cried because of it."

Buck smiled. "She wasn't crying because of me. She was thinking about her future grandbaby."

Chapter 27

⎯⌇⊚⌇⎯

Buck spent much of the next day worrying about his impending fatherhood. He worked in the barn, playing with Pard, grooming the horses and getting in Hector's way until the little man with dark hair and big smile grabbed his elbow.

"Want to tell me what is wrong?"

"What makes you think something is wrong?"

"Because you are following me around like a sick colt. Now, either go away and leave me alone, or tell me your problem."

Hector smiled when Buck said, "I'm going to be a father."

"Wonderful." The smile disappeared from his face and he said, "But you are not married, are you?"

Buck shook his head. "Not even close."

Hector led him to a chair in the barn, sat him down and then stood before him in a lecturing posture. Buck realized what he was about to hear would not be complimentary.

"Did you get a girl pregnant accidentally?"

"I wasn't really thinking about it if that's what you mean."

Hector shook his head and frowned, revealing the gap in his front teeth. "You have to make this right.

What you did is a sin. You have to marry the girl."

Hector's dark eyes grew even larger when Buck said, "I think she is already married."

When Buck explained, Hector became very agitated and began talking in Spanish. Then he yelled for LaDona who came running out of the house to check on the commotion. After a lengthy and animated conversation in Spanish, the two turned to Buck, glaring at him.

"You must see the Priest," she said. "He'll know what to do."

Buck seriously doubted he would, especially once he told him the mother-to-be was a practicing member of the Southern Death Cult religion. He decided to withhold that tidbit of information from Hector and LaDona, as they were already very upset. He finally promised them he would speak with Father Sanchez. The pledge failed to assuage his feelings, but earned him supportive smiles from the couple.

What Buck needed, he realized, was a healing ride on his pony. Lady was more than ready for him, snorting and moving her head as he saddled and bridled her. The ride was what they both needed and two hours had passed when they trotted back to the barn, Pard wagging his tail as he followed along behind.

They found Kristy's Prius parked in front of the barn but she was not in it. She was sitting on the porch with Hector and LaDona. They were all laughing, LaDona hugging her. She had obviously made a good impression on the couple because Hector pumped his hand.

"Kristy is a wonderful woman. You are a lucky man."

Glancing at Kristy, he said, "I have to hose Lady down and settle her."

"Take your time. We're having a nice visit."

Buck was brushing Lady's mane when Kristy

joined him in the stall. Lady and Pard took to her immediately.

"She is such a beautiful animal. I have never touched a horse before now."

"You have to be kidding. You grew up in Oklahoma and have never touched a horse?"

Kristy smiled and nodded. "Not Oklahoma; Texas. I don't know why; I just never had the opportunity. I'd love to ride her."

It was Buck's turn to smile. "I think I can arrange it."

"Great, then it's a date."

Kristy grabbed Buck's hand, stood on her tiptoes and kissed him.

"Is everything okay?" he asked, again wondering about the purpose of Kristy's visit.

"Everything is wonderful. I just thought I would take a drive and see where you live. I was curious."

"Come upstairs and I'll show you."

Buck gave her a quick tour of his apartment, pointing out the Oriental rugs, wood floors and demonstrating the gold-plated faucets.

"Ooh, this is wonderful. I didn't realize you were so wealthy."

"I'm not, but my landlady is. I help out around the place in exchange for free board for Lady, Pard and me."

"What kind of help?" Kristy asked.

"If I didn't know better, I'd think you are jealous."

"Do I need to be?"

She smiled when he said, "Not as long as I stay away from Lana's ceremonial pipe."

Kristy sank into one of his overstuffed chairs as he showered and changed into fresh clothes. Then he took her to a nice restaurant in Guthrie in his new Maroon Navigator.

"Will you stay the night?" he asked when they returned from dinner.

Kristy answered him with a smile and squeeze of his hand. Later, they lay in his bed.

"I've done lots of thinking about this child thing," he said.

"I knew you had."

"How could you tell?"

"You don't cover your emotions very well."

"Then maybe you know what I'm thinking now."

Kristy giggled. "I have a good idea."

"Not that. I was thinking maybe you and I could get married and you could help me raise the kid, if I can get it from Lana."

Kristy pulled away, turned and faced him. The light was dim but he could see she was no longer smiling.

"I love you but marriage is out of the question. Lykaia is my place in the world. I have a purpose there."

"And I'm not part of your purpose?"

"You have a purpose of your own. You can't just simply deal with the upcoming birth of your child by marrying someone indiscriminately and thinking it will solve your problem."

"What can I do? I feel helpless and it's not a feeling I like."

Kristy caressed his neck. "Things will work out, I promise, and Esme and I will always be here for you."

Chapter 28

"What's taking so long?" Clayton O'Meara asked as he paced around the table.

"Knock it off, Clay. You are not even supposed to be here, remember?" Sheriff Hagen said.

The windowless room was abuzz with activity, television screens and computer monitors flickering as several uniformed operators entered data from their keyboards. Five men, including Sheriff Hagen, sat around a conference table strewn with maps and activity reports. Two of the men wore suits marking them as OSBI.

"This place gives me the creeps. It reminds me of something out of the Cold War."

"Quit belly-aching, O'Meara. There are some of us here that actually participated in the Cold War."

Agent Gray Norman's words caused Clayton to frown and glance at his watch again. Taller and older than Clayton, Norman's expensive suit and well-coiffed white hair marked him as someone near the pinnacle of the Bureau's hierarchy. His younger partner seemed uncowed by his stature.

"Twenty minutes and counting," the younger man said as he snapped shut his flip phone and glanced at the television screen.

Harold Taylor's cheap suit marked him as a junior agent although his height was no less impressive than Norman's, his shoulder's as wide as a tight end for the Dallas Cowboys.

"Lucifer Jameson's limo is pulling into the compound grounds."

Clayton asked, "Who is he and what's his importance?"

"From what we know, he's the head man at Molasse. He rarely leaves Australia so this must be an important visit. There's a big party going on to impress him."

"What kind of parents would name their son Lucifer?" Clayton asked.

"Apparently a father named Lucifer," Gray Norman said.

Sheriff Hagen fidgeted with a pencil. "His name fits him. He's suspected of everything from drug trafficking to murder but no one's pinned anything on him yet."

Gray Norman stood and faced Clayton when he said, "What are we paying you people for if you can't even control a thug like him?"

"I don't like your attitude, O'Meara."

"Yeah, well what are you going to do about it?"

"Maybe I'll kick your ass."

"You and what army?"

"I don't need an army and I think you have an overblown opinion of yourself."

Captain Dave Warren, the Logan County second-in-command interrupted the two squabbling men.

"Gentlemen, we are about to go live. I suggest you settle your differences later, unless you want them aired across Oklahoma."

Gray Norman returned to his chair, as did Clayton.

Several TV screens suddenly came alive, focusing on police and plain-clothes cops occupying similar rooms, somewhere in other counties.

"It's a go here in Seminole County."

"Lincoln County is ready."

"Ditto, Cleveland."

The camera focused on Sheriff Hagen. "I'm Jim Hagen, Sheriff of Logan County. Our SWAT team is in place outside the compound north of Crescent, but there is a delay. We are on hold for Operation Race Horse to begin.

Someone from another county was getting antsy. "What's the delay?"

"A tall fence surrounds the compound and there is a guard at the gate. From our surveillance, we have learned the operation's supervisor, driving an armored Hummer, reports to the compound every night around ten. He's running late, probably because of the party in progress."

"What's the significance of the Hummer?"

"Our team is in hiding across the road. They plan to follow the vehicle into the compound once the guard opens the gate, and then dispatching him with a tranquilizer dart."

Can't they accomplish the same thing without the Hummer, and climb the fence?"

'They could, but we think the gate and fence have sensors that would send an alarm to the house and spoil our surprise."

"Then what do we do?"

"We wait."

***

A SWAT team comprised of police officers from Logan and Oklahoma Counties waited across from the gated compound, a lavish party in full swing at the house on the hill. The team had hiked through the woods, cross-country to their present location. The single road leading to the compound had been constantly guarded since Buck and Trey's visit.

Thirty men dressed in camouflage fatigues and

dark hoods sprawled on their stomachs, waiting for the arrival of a black Hummer. A horsefly buzzed around Buck's head as sweat trickled down his face. The cross-country trek had tired him, making his bulletproof vest feel extra constricting.

He had removed the backpack he'd used to carry water and extra ammunition on their trek. Once the attack began, he would no longer need it. Another half-hour passed before they heard the rumbling of the heavy Hummer coming down the road. Every man along the row grew ready.

When the guard recognized the black vehicle, the heavy gate began opening slowly. As it did, a SWAT team sharpshooter ran behind the Hummer. When the dark vehicle headed up the landscaped pathway to the large house on the hill, the sniper dispatched the guard with a single tranquilizer dart to his neck.

The sergeant in command said, "Move out, single file."

Buck waited until the man in front of him entered the open gate of the compound before following him across the rural road. Headphones connected the team, although they needed little prompting to carry out the well-rehearsed operation. The SWAT unit moved toward the mansion by way of advancing shadows. Within minutes, they had the large structure cordoned. Still undetected, they awaited orders.

The noisy party, along with many guests moving in and out of the house, compromised the guards at the doors. Fifty or more boisterous visitors carried on outside by the pool. A band played and drinks flowed liberally. Another fifty police officers awaited word the assault had begun. Disguised as church members in buses, they turned off Highway 74, onto the road to the compound moments after the first wave compromised the front gate.

Sharp shooters soon identified their targets. When the lead sergeant gave the command, they took out their respective targets with tranquilizer darts and then began advancing on the mansion. Buck was among the first to enter and found a raucous party in progress. A collision with a security guard jarred his headphone loose, knocking it across the floor.

The orchestra, security guards and partiers grew quiet when the SWAT team appeared, automatic weapons drawn and ready. Buck loosened himself from the stunned security guard when he saw someone coming down the stairs he recognized. The sight of her almost caused him to stop dead in his tracks.

Chapter 29

It was Georgia, apparently quite dazed from the way she clutched the banister. Tears streaked her makeup, her hair a mess. Someone had ripped the front of her pink party gown and it was covered in blood. She also had black eyes and swollen lips. Although she clutched the torn bodice, her efforts did little to cover her exposed breasts, grown red with blood. Buck's dark mask frightened her and she backed against the banister.

"It's me," he said, uncovering his face to show her who he was. "Are you all right?"

"This isn't my blood, if that's what you mean," she said, hugging him.

"You have to find a place to hide, or you'll be arrested."

"I can't go back upstairs. Roy will kill me."

"Is he alone?"

"He's with Jimmy Quick and a man with an Australian accent. They tried to force me to have sex with them. I stabbed the Aussie in the leg with a ceremonial dagger Roy keeps on his desk as a letter opener. I must have struck a vein or artery because blood began gushing everywhere."

Buck glanced around, looking for someone to help

him, wondering if he had time to go downstairs and call for backup.

"Is there another way out of the house?"

Georgia nodded. "A secret passage. I saw Roy go in it once. He bloodied my lip and told me to forget about it if I knew what was good for me."

"Take me to it," he said.

Shouts from SWAT team members, along with general chaos, confusion and vocal protests of arrested guests died away as they hurried upstairs, finding Roy's office door ajar. The lavishly decorated room was empty.

Georgia pointed. "The passage is behind that panel but I don't know how to open it."

Buck began feeling the wall, hoping to find the opening mechanism. Finally, he kicked a hole in it with his boot and crawled through.

"Wait on me," Georgia said.

"Too dangerous. Stay here."

"No way," she said, following him through the hole, into the darkness.

Buck groped for a light switch. Finding none, he began descending the circular staircase, Georgia clutching the back of his shirt. Within minutes, they saw a light up ahead—a small fluorescent bulb above a closed door.

"On the ground," he said.

Finding the door locked, Buck blasted it with his assault rifle. When he kicked it open, he stared into the startled eyes of Jimmy Quick. Before he could react, Quick unloaded his 9 mm Glock, bullets wheeling him around. Losing his footing, he fell backwards, onto the cement floor. Jimmy Quick was on him in an instant, ripping off his black mask.

"You mother fucker! I should have known it was you."

Quick pointed the pistol between Buck's eyes. For a moment, he thought he was a dead man, but Quick had other ideas.

"A bullet through the brain is too easy for you. This won't be our last meeting. Next time I'll take my time and make you wish I'd already killed you."

Instead of shooting him, Quick kicked Buck in the head and then hurried away down the darkened hallway. Dazed but conscious, he lay in a stupor until a crying Georgia lifted his head and rubbed his cheek.

"Oh my God, Buck! Please don't be dead."

He shook the cobwebs from his head and prodded the tender spots beneath the bulletproof vest with his fingers.

"My vest saved me. Help me up."

Georgia's tears grew heavier as she pulled him into a sitting position. He winced, fearing broken ribs when she hugged him.

"Let's get out of here," she said.

Georgia turned and took a step toward the spot where Buck had first seen Jimmy Quick.

"Wait!" he yelled as an explosion rocked the darkness behind them.

Quick had armed a booby trap, destroying a large part of the secret passageway. Acrid smoke began filling the narrow hall as Buck realized there was now only one way out. Georgia no longer made any pretense of trying to hide her bloody breasts. It didn't matter because Buck had other things on his mind, namely survival. His ribs hurt like hell, but a steady surge of adrenaline into his bloodstream got him moving again. Unbuttoning his camouflage shirt, he removed his bulletproof vest, handing Georgia the shirt. She put it on and they started forward at a rapid clip.

"I can't wait on you," he finally said.

"I run 10 Ks. You'll probably have trouble keeping up with me."

"Then come on," he said, sprinting down the dimly lit hallway.

Her pink party dress in shambles, Georgia

matched Buck stride for stride. When they reached the end of the tunnel, they heard the sound of a revving airplane engine. Pushing open a heavy door, they watched as Jimmy Quick's blue pickup truck kicked up a plume of dust and disappeared down a dirt road.

The tunnel had led them to a spot some distance from the compound. A short dirt runway extended from a hanger, hidden from above by camouflaged netting. A red windsock was the only indication the dusty area was anything more than a horse pasture.

A very small two-seater plane had taxied to the other end of the runway, apparently to take advantage of a steady tail wind. Realizing it was Roy and Lucifer making their escape, Buck dropped to a prone position on the runway, pointed his H & K MP5 assault rifle at the plane's engine block and opened fire. Three well-placed bullets found a cylinder, causing the engine to seize. The plane was moving fast. Even though it would never leave the ground, it continued rushing toward him.

Buck emptied the rest of the thirty-round clip into the wheels and struts. As if in slow motion, the little plane nosed into the ground and skidded to a halt, coating him with oil, dirt and smoke. One of the plane's doors opened and Roy Dunlap rolled out, raising his arms when he saw the weapon pointed at him. Intent on the wounded Australian in the smoking plane, Buck popped in another clip, and then handed the MP5 to Georgia.

"Kill him if he makes a move."

Georgia looked a mess, her hair beyond mussed and her party dress in tatters. With her finger on the trigger, she pointed the assault weapon at Dunlap, her angry stare daring him to move. Buck ran to the passenger side of the plane, forced open the door and pulled the injured Lucifer Jameson to safety.

Either Dunlap or Quick had tied a tourniquet around Jameson's thigh. It had probably kept him from bleeding to death but he was in poor shape when Buck pulled him away from the smoking plane and laid him on the ground.

He didn't have to wonder how they would get the injured man back to the compound as a half dozen SWAT team members soon joined them. An ambulance also arrived, along with a police cruiser. He and Georgia were returned to the grounds of the compound where the operation was mopping up, loading people into buses with barred windows. One of the deputies grabbed Georgia's elbow and directed her to get in line. Buck gave the man a shove, facing him when he wheeled around.

"She's not going to County with the others."

The man had already worked himself into a serious state of anger, his frowning face visibly red, even in dim moonlight.

He was spitting when he said, "Our orders are to bring everyone in, which means in the bus."

"No way. She's a material witness and her life wouldn't be worth a plug nickel."

The man's nametag said Deputy Brewster, Oklahoma County. He had the build of a weight lifter and the shaved head of a person who took his job in law enforcement seriously. With his hand on his service revolver, he got into Buck's face.

"You're overstepping your authority. You're not even a real cop."

Buck showed him his badge. "Not only am I sworn in, I'm a Logan County deputy. In case you forgot, we're in Logan, not Oklahoma County. Now take your hands off the woman."

"You want a piece of my ass, I'll be happy to oblige you," the Oklahoma County deputy said, edging closer to Buck's face.

By now, a crowd had gathered, forming a circle around the two men. It was then the officer in charge stepped forward. Sergeant Lawson was as young as

Buck and as big as Brewster. Unlike Brewster, his own dark eyes were introspective and not angry. One of Sheriff Hagen's key men, he knew Buck and was aware of his relationship with the Sheriff.

"What's going on here?" he said, stepping between Buck and Brewster.

"This woman isn't guilty of anything and she's a key witness in this case. She would be in mortal danger if she gets on the bus with everyone else."

"Most of the guests are probably not guilty of anything. It doesn't matter. They all go on the bus. We have officers watching the situation. She goes with them. Understand?"

Buck popped the clip into his MP5 and took a step backwards. "Over my dead body."

"You want to die because of this woman?" Sergeant Lawson asked.

"Do you?"

Seeing things were out of hand, Lawson glanced at the armed officers behind him, raised his hand and shook his head.

"Just be cool. I'm calling Sheriff Hagen."

Explaining the situation to the Sheriff, he cautiously handed the cell phone to Buck.

"What in the cornbread hell is going on out there? Put the woman on the bus and get your ass in here. Now!"

"No can do, Sheriff."

"This is procedure and you need to follow it. Put your weapon down."

"Let me talk to Clayton first."

Thinking he had diffused the stand off, he handed the phone to Clayton.

"I have Georgia with me. She stabbed Lucifer when he and Jimmy Quick tried to rape her. She'll be in danger, maybe even killed if she gets in one of those buses."

"Hold the phone," he said, turning to Sheriff

Hagen, and Agents Norman and Taylor. "Gentlemen, the woman Buck is protecting is Georgia Goetty, an employee of mine for at least ten years. McDivit is also my employee and he believes she would be in grave danger if she gets on one of the buses. I think so too."

"What do you suggest we do then, O'Meara?" Agent Norman asked.

"The President and the last three Presidents are all personal friends of mine. I'm not suggesting anything, I'm telling you. If one hair on the woman's head is harmed, or Buck McDivit's, I'm going to personally see to it everyone in this room is busted back to the same rank they were the day they started. Now, someone had better make a quick and sane decision here or I'm going to start making phone calls."

Clayton returned the phone to Sheriff Hagen, walked across the room and poured a cup of coffee.

"Put Sergeant Lawson back on the line."

"Yes Sir," Lawson said.

"Get the buses moving. You stay with Buck and the woman until I get there."

"But . . ."

"You have your orders, Sergeant. They require no explanation. Are you clear on this?"

Lawson had no time to reply because Sheriff Hagen slammed his cell phone shut.

Chapter 30

Buck lay in Esme's teepee, trying not to grimace as the gorgeous woman administered a poultice to the three purple bruises which colored his chest. Beauty licked his hand and he stroked her long muzzle.

"You are beginning to perturb me, Buck McDivit. I've only known you a short while and I've already lost count of the times you've needed critical care."

She frowned and shook her head when he said, "I usually go a year or more between major wounds."

"It's not funny. I'm worried about Quick. He's tried to kill you three times already. Next time you might not be so lucky."

"He's probably in Mexico by now. If he is still in Logan County, the Sheriff will track him down. Too many people know him."

"I might have believed it a week ago. Now, I'm not so sure. Will you stay with me tonight?"

"There's no place I'd rather be, but I have a meeting with Sheriff Hagen and the OSBI first thing tomorrow."

"You could leave from here. I'll get you up."

Buck smiled at her double entendre. "My notes are back at Sunset Farms and Trey is picking me up at six."

Esme rustled through a small cabinet, returning

with a necklace bearing a gold pendant in the shape of the same rattlesnake image as the tattoo on her shoulder. She put it around his neck and clasped it.

"You must promise me you won't take this off."

"What is it?"

"A powerful talisman. Nothing can protect you if the Great Spirit deems it so, but it will ward off most evil spirits. Promise me you won't remove it."

"The authorities will think I'm crazy."

"Promise me."

Buck bent forward and kissed her. "Evil spirits will have to rip it from my dying body."

Esme squeezed his hand and shook her head. "Don't joke about things like this. I would feel lots better if you took Beauty with you."

"I can't take her to the meeting. I'll be fine, I promise."

When Esme kissed him, tears filled her eyes. "I must take a journey and I may never see you again."

"What are you talking about?"

She didn't answer him, instead, speaking something in an unfamiliar language, and then waiting by the flap of the teepee.

"The sound of danger is singing in my brain and I can't make it stop. Go now, but sleep with an ear to the ground and one eye open."

***

Buck's new Navigator waited at Lykaia's front gate where Kristy dropped him off.

"You be careful, Buck McDivit. I don't think I could go on living if something were to happen to you."

"Stop it. Esme has me spooked enough as it is."

"It's because we love you."

"I love you too and I'll be fine. I'll be back tomorrow night."

The sky was dark as Buck exited the commune and entered the thick covering of trees leading back to the nearest section line road. He had traveled less than a tenth of a mile when a blue pickup burst from the darkness and nailed into the Navigator's right front fender, powering it into the ditch. Jimmy Quick was on him as he opened the door, tossing a noose around his neck and yanking.

Buck rolled out of the cab, onto the ground, as Quick pulled hard on the rope. Struggling to catch his breath, he caught the hilt of Quick's heavy hunting knife across his temple. It was the last thing he remembered for a while.

Chapter 31

Buck's head throbbed when he opened his eyes, finding himself naked and lying on his back in damp sand. A man stood over him and he could see clearly in the dim fluorescence of a camping lantern it was Jimmy Quick. When he tried to rise, he realized his hands were tied behind his back. A knife cut oozing blood extended from his breastbone to just below his belly button.

"You are about to die, McDivit, but first I'm going to make you beg me to kill you."

Buck's blood had already attracted mosquitoes and horseflies. They flittered in and out of his wound. Unable to swat them away, he tried to ignore them, knowing he had much deeper concerns to worry about.

"In case you think someone might come to your rescue before I kill you, better think again. Your Lincoln is in the creek, out of sight from the road. They won't find your bones until next spring."

Seeing the magic talisman around Buck's neck, Quick yanked it, breaking the string and dropping it to the sand beside him.

"Nice try. Someone very powerful is watching out for you and they'll be upset when they find your rotting carcass."

Buck struggled to loosen his wrists bound with baling wire and it was working. His feet were free and when Quick bent forward to cut him, he kicked him in the groin. After a grimace and a groan, Quick slapped Buck hard and then held the knife to his throat.

"You hold still. I don't want to kill you just yet, but I will if I have to."

With the knife at Buck's neck, Quick wrapped baling wire around his ankles and knees. When he had him more secure, he took another slice with his knife, this one parallel to the first. Buck kept his mouth shut, not giving Quick the satisfaction the knife wounds had hurt him.

"You ain't yelling enough. Maybe you need a little fist first."

Quick began pummeling Buck's face with the flat of his hand, continuing until his eyes had swelled shut and blood trickled from his nose and lips. Despite the beating, Buck refused to moan, cry out, or show any emotion at all. It earned him a kick in the ribs with the toe of Quick's boot.

"I'm going to skin you alive, starting at your neck. If you cry for me, I might be merciful and kill you a little early, but then again, maybe not. Oh, and I'm not forgetting about your balls and dick. They'll be gone long before you die."

Quick began a precise incision along Buck's left shoulder blade, moving slowly. He was about to gnaw away the skin on the inside of his mouth, wincing from pain but determined not to give Quick the satisfaction. All his senses heightened, he heard something moving stealthily behind the lunatic with the knife. It was coming toward them and Buck knew without seeing it was the panther. He braced for the attack, figuring death by the big black cat would be a quicker and less painful alternative. He didn't have long to wait.

The panther lunged, landing on Jimmy Quick's shoulders and powering him onto Buck's chest. With its fangs buried in Quick's neck, the big cat shook his victim like a rag doll. Already dead, Quick's lifeless eyes stared at Buck as the animal dragged him into the thick undergrowth of vegetation encompassing Skeleton Creek. Buck soon fell into a stupor, passing out from a combination of the beating and loss of blood. The panther didn't return.

***

When Buck opened his eyes, he saw Esme kneeling beside him, Beauty by her side.

"I was so worried. Beauty awoke me and demanded I follow her. She led me here. Did Quick do this to you?"

"Get me loose and I'll tell you."

Esme stroked the cut across his shoulder blade and then undid the baling wire around his knees and ankles.

"Why did you remove the talisman? You promised me you wouldn't take it off."

Buck didn't answer. When she rolled him over to release his wrists, she saw the remains of the necklace and the rattlesnake pendant clutched in his hands.

"Quick ripped it off of my neck, but I didn't let it get far away."

Beauty licked his face as Esme kissed him. "I'm glad you are alive but I am tiring of the constant doctoring you seem to require."

Buck smiled. "Just once more and I promise, I'll be more careful from now on."

Chapter 32

Buck's wounds were almost healed when he rode Lady to Clayton's ranch, Pard following closely behind. A small party was in progress on Clayton's veranda. Trey and Beth, and Jim and Carol Hagen had joined Clayton and KK for the occasion. Maria smiled and shook her head when Buck requested coffee, black, soon returning instead with a pitcher of margaritas.

"We were starting to get worried," Clayton said. "Glad you could make it."

Seeing the forlorn expression on the young cowboy's face, Beth asked, "Buck, are you okay?"

"Just a little sad."

Clayton grinned. "What's the matter? You look like you just lost your favorite puppy."

Jim and Carol already knew what the matter was. Esme and Beauty had departed Lykaia, perhaps forever. In grief, Kristy had also left the compound to return to her parent's home in Austin.

"I'm okay. The past few weeks have just put me into a bit of a funk, but I'll be fine. Don't let me spoil the party."

Beth, Carol and KK couldn't bear Buck's unhappy expression. Descending on him like mothers whose child had just stubbed his toe, they proceeded to console him with kisses and hugs.

"My own mother never gave me that kind of attention," Trey said, shaking his head.

Jim agreed. "Neither did mine."

"Hey, at least you two had mothers," Clayton said, grinning at his little joke.

Buck detached himself from the three doting women and settled into a chair with the group, all of them well beyond their first pitcher of margaritas.

"You really made a mess of the last Navigator I gave you. I think I'm going to have to cut you back to an economy class vehicle."

"You don't need me any more. Keep your car."

"You're wrong. I realize now I need a full-time security officer and I can think of no one better for the job than you."

"No offense, Clayton, but you know I've never been happy working full time for anyone, and you fleshed out my bank account to the point I don't need to. If I were married and had kids to worry about, it might be a different story. Guess it's never going to happen."

Hearing the hurt in his voice, Carol patted his hand. "You are young and I still expect at least one grandchild before I turn sixty."

"You'll both get what you want," Clayton said. "I have an announcement to make. I'm getting married."

Beth and Carol hugged Clayton, and then KK, as Sheriff Hagen, Buck and Trey pumped Clayton's hand.

"We are so happy for you two," Beth said.

Clayton glanced at KK and they both laughed. "Not KK," he said, "Lana."

"You are marrying Lana?" Beth blurted.

Clayton held up a placating palm. "It's really no more than a marriage of convenience which will benefit both Lykaia and O'Meara."

"But what about KK?" Carol asked, pointedly.

"We are a couple and already have a civil union. We'll never separate. Tell them, KK."

"I'm not the jealous type. Clayton can spend as much time at Lykaia as he wants, as long as he takes me with him."

"And this union has a benefit for you, Buck," Clayton said. "We'll have custody of your child at least half of the time. You can interact with him as much as you want. When you are comfortable letting him know you are his father, we'll see to it that it happens."

"What about me?" Carol asked.

"You're in, Grandma," Clayton said with a smile. "This is a win, win situation."

Maria interrupted their banter with yet another pitcher of margaritas.

"Don't anyone worry about driving home. I have more rooms in this place than a hotel and KK and I love guests. Drink up!"

The honking of a truck horn outside the veranda suddenly riveted everyone's attention. Satchel and Georgia didn't bother knocking as they joined the party.

"You two come in this house," Clayton said. "Maria, we have more guests."

Both dressed in worn jeans, cowboy boots and colorful Western shirts, Satchel and Georgia looked happier than Buck could remember seeing either of them. They had mile-wide grins.

"What about you two?" Sheriff Hagen asked. "Is there a wedding in your future?"

"We're just having a good time, Brother," Satchel said, clutching Georgia even closer.

Georgia continued to smile. "I'm in love with this big galoot and I have Buck to thank."

Satchel agreed. "We both have Buck to thank."

***

The party continued into the night, Trey and Buck finally ducking outside for a talk. The sky was luminous, filled with stars and the bright light of a full moon. Trey gave Buck a high five.

"We did it, my friend. We busted the biggest cattle-rustling ring this state has ever seen. It earned me a big promotion and Beth and I are also getting married."

"Good for you," Buck said.

"What about Kristy? She's a real looker and I can tell she really likes you."

Buck had an arm around Pard and scratched one of his ears as he talked.

"She was heart-broken when Esme and Beauty left Lykaia. Lana says she went back to Austin."

"Where did Esme go?"

Buck could only shake his head. "She said she had a journey to take. I don't know why, or where to."

Trey patted Buck's shoulder. "You are young and have more gorgeous women hanging around than anyone I know."

"I'm just so depressed. I never had parents and now I have lost Esme, Beauty and Kristy. It's just not fair."

Trey grinned. "You still have me and Beth, and don't forget about Pard and Lady, and Jim and Carol. Tell you the truth, I'm having a hard time feeling sorry for you."

Buck smiled. "You're right. Pard is a wonderful dog and Lady the most forgiving female I ever met."

"You're worried about your son, aren't you?"

"I'd be lying if I said I'm not. I know Lana, Clayton and KK have his best interest at heart, but I don't like the idea of playing second-fiddle as a father."

Trey slapped his shoulder. "He'll be fine. You are, and you never had a dad, much less two."

Unable to contain himself, Buck put his arms around Trey and hugged him. "At least I have a brother."

Trey pushed him away. "Quit dribbling on my shoulder or I'm going to have to whack you."

Buck grinned. "I guess we did bust the biggest

cattle-rustling ring in Oklahoma history."

"You bet your sweet ass we did, even if you had to tell one whopper of a lie to get it done."

"My butt was puckered for awhile, but everything worked out. Still, I don't feel right taking money from Clayton, even though he does have more gold than Midas."

"Have him put you on retainer. Then you can help him whenever he needs it, and you'll have your freedom in the meantime."

"Maybe," Buck said. "I'll have to think about it, but I am getting attached to big Navigator's."

"What else? Are you going to be okay?"

"I'll make it, but Pard and me may have to take a trip."

"Where to?"

"It's been a long time since I visited Austin and someone is there I think has a few answers to the questions I have. Maybe she is missing someone as much as I am. I need to find out."

Trey just nodded. Clouds momentarily cloaked the Oklahoma landscape. When the full moon emerged, it lighted the surroundings, its appearance accompanied by the mournful howl of a distant wolf. Trey didn't know what to make of it, but Buck smiled.

He knew.

END

Eric Wilder

241

Eric Wilder grew up a mile from Black Bayou in northwest Louisiana. After earning degrees in geology, and a stint in Vietnam, he moved to Oklahoma. He now lives and writes in Edmond, Oklahoma, along with wife Marilyn, daughter Kate, three dogs and a cat named Goldie. Please visit him at EricWilder.com.

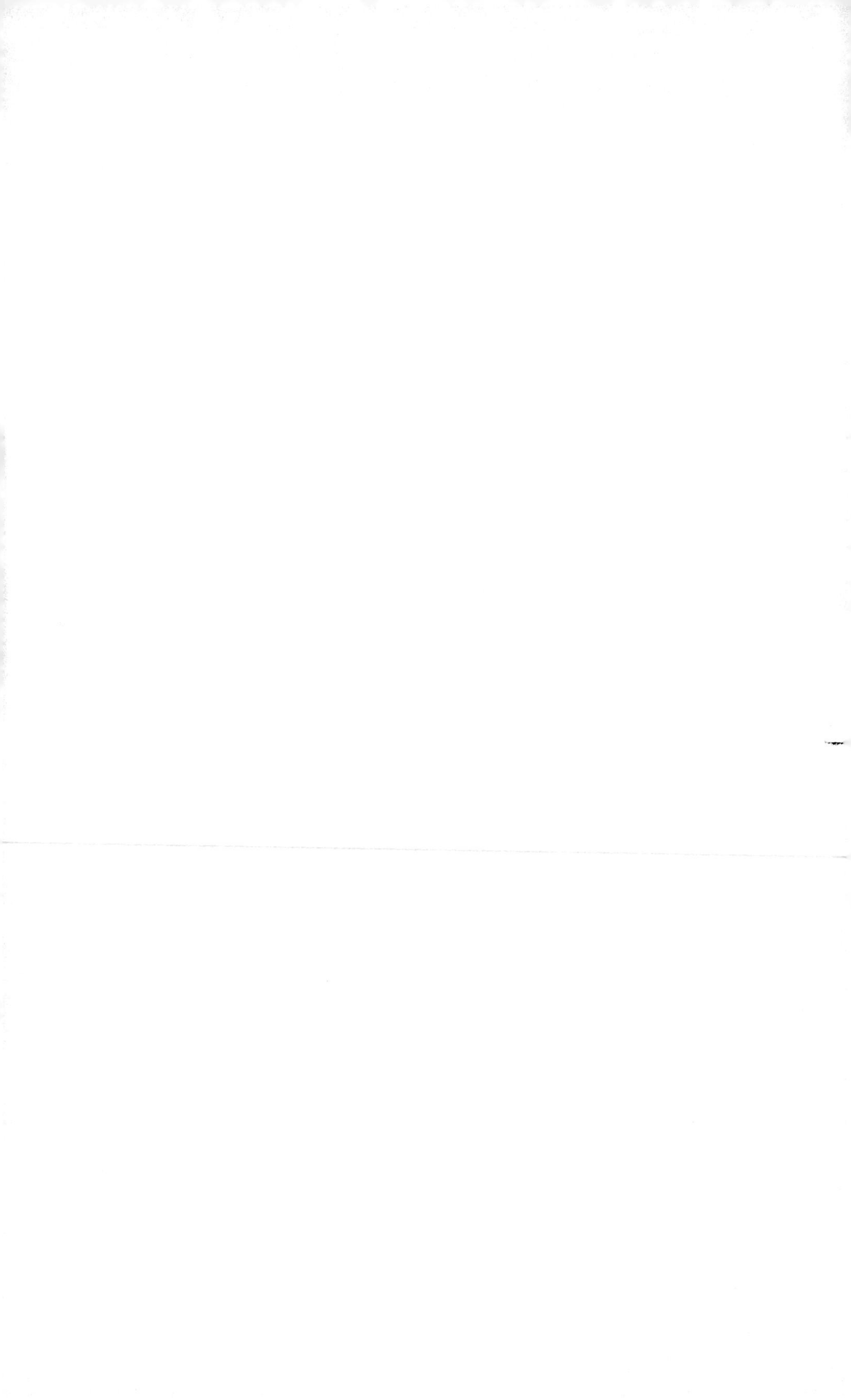